ACADEMY OF THE FOUND

RESURRECTING MAGIC - BOOK FOUR

KEARY TAYLOR

Copyright © 2020 Keary Taylor
All rights reserved. Except as permitted under the U.S. Copyright act of 1976, no part of this publication may be reproduced, distributed, or transmitted in any form or by any means, or stored in a database or retrieval system, without the prior written permission of the author.

First Edition: October 2020

Cover art by Orina Kafe

The characters and events portrayed in this book are fictitious. Any similarity to real persons, living or dead, is coincidental and not intended by the author.

Taylor, Keary, 1987-

Academy of the Found (Resurrecting Magic): a novel / by Keary Taylor.
— 1st ed.

ALSO BY KEARY TAYLOR

RESURRECTING MAGIC SERIES

Rise of the Mage

Keeper of the Lost

Shadow of the Locked

Academy of the Found

THE BLOOD DESCENDANTS UNIVERSE

House of Royals Saga

House of Royals

House of Pawns

House of Kings

House of Judges

House of Ravens

Garden of Thorns Trilogy

Garden of Thorns

Garden of Snakes

Garden of Graves

Crown of Death Saga

Crown of Death

Crown of Blood

Crown of Ruin

Crown of Bones

THE FALL OF ANGELS TRILOGY

Branded

Forsaken

Vindicated

Afterlife (the novelette companion to Vindicated)

Returned (ten year anniversary follow up)

THE EDEN TRILOGY

The Raid (An Eden Short Story)

The Ashes (an Eden Prequel)

The Bane (Book 1)

The Human (Book 2)

The Eve (Book 3)

THE NERON RISING SAGA

Neron Rising

Neron Skies

Nero Awakening

Nero Blood

Nero Nights

Neron Wars

Nero Kingdom

THE McCAIN SAGA

Ever After Drake

Moments of Julian

Depths of Lake

Playing it Kale

WHAT I DIDN'T SAY

Also by T.L. Keary (thriller/suspense pen name)

THREE HEART ECHO

OUR LAST CONFESSION

SKIN AND BONE

CHAPTER ONE

When I imagined this moment in my head, I didn't hesitate. I ran right up to her. I embraced her so tight that both our bones threatened to crack. We both sobbed and we'd laughed and cried some more, and the moment was filled with magic.

Instead, I found myself frozen in place, and my entire body cold with absolute disbelief.

Five years. It had been five years.

In my heart, I had always held on to hope. But in my brain, I knew the reasonable explanation. That after five years, logically, she must be dead.

Logic and reality were clashing. So, I stared at my mother like I was seeing a ghost.

She held my eyes, which were the same shade of blue as her own, and I wondered if I looked like a ghost as well. I was only fifteen when she disappeared. And now here I was, grown into a woman. I might have still looked like her little girl in my features, but the details had surely changed.

"Are you alright?"

Nathaniel's voice was soft and even in my ear. It held a million degrees of support and concern.

"Margot?"

My father's voice was confused and perhaps a little bit disappointed.

Because we'd been through all of this together. Just the two of us. Surviving her disappearance. The investigation into him as a suspect. Together, we'd held on to the hope that someday she would return. And now here she was, standing right in front of me, and I couldn't say a word. I didn't even feel able to move.

"I am so sorry," Mom said. And with her words, just the four of them, the cold, protective ice in me began to crack a little. "I'm so sorry, Margot." She took a slow step forward. "I'm so sorry I didn't explain everything sooner. I tried to protect you too much, but you're you, Margot. You could have handled it. I'm so sorry I wasn't more careful. I'm so sorry for the past five years."

I didn't need an apology. I'd never once considered it.

But...maybe I did.

Because with her words, that unknown, cold part of me fractured into a million pieces. All the emotions I'd held onto for the past five years brimmed up inside of me and tears instantly welled in my eyes. And I took those last two steps and threw my arms around my mother.

"Mom," I said into her neck. And it all came flooding back to me. I remembered what it was like to have a mother to cling to. A woman to hold me up when I was fracturing and needed support. I remembered what it was like to stay up late at night, talking to her about nothing and everything. I remembered running down the beach, wind blowing in our hair, screaming in delight at nothing more than the sunshine.

And here she was, returned to me.

"I'm so sorry, baby girl," she said as she ran her hand down the back of my hair.

I shook my head and pulled back so that I could look at her.

The evidence of time was there on her face. I didn't remember those crows' feet around her eyes being so deep. I didn't remember her skin looking so weathered. I didn't remember her eyes looking so haunted.

"How?" I asked, and the word came out in a hoarse crack.

She clung to me and stared into my eyes. And I finally understood it, just how much I looked like her. People had always told me I did. We had the same dirty blonde hair. The same blue eyes, same button shaped nose, and the same cheekbones.

"It's a long story, my love," she said, offering me a

smile. "Why don't you introduce me to your friends first?"

I was in a hurry to get answers, so introductions were the last thing I wanted to bother with. But I understood why it was important for them to happen. Before she could share what happened to her, she needed to know if it was safe to talk in front of the crowd that was behind me.

"Mom, this is an extension of my family," I said. My eyes cast over them, and they each stared at my mother with a range of reactions. Not all of them knew the history. Some knew it quite well. "This is Marie and Julie Daniels. And Peter Wills. They're students at our school."

I watched my mother's expression change in reaction to those last few words. There was so much catching up to do. "And Poppy Gowens. Mary-Beth Foster. Borden Stewart."

Each of them gave a nod of the head or a wave as I said their names. Mary-Beth looked as if she was going to burst from holding in all the emotions and words she was experiencing right now. Borden just kept looking back at me, gauging my reaction to this new situation. Poppy knew very little about the situation with my mother.

"And," I said, my heart beginning to race as my eyes slid over to the man standing by my side, "this is my fiancé, Nathaniel Nightingale."

It was actually kind of fun, watching Mom's reaction to that sentence. Her eyes grew wide. She looked from me, to Nathaniel, back to me, down to the ring on my finger, and then back to my dad.

"You didn't think to mention on our way over here that our daughter is *engaged*?" she demanded.

It might not have been about them, but no one in the house could stop themselves from laughing at Mom's reaction.

"There are more than a few things to bring you up to speed on, my darling," my dad said with a chuckle.

"This is kind of one of those big things," Mom said with a disbelieving laugh as she turned back around.

"It's an absolute honor to get to meet you, Amelia Bell," Nathaniel said with a wonder-filled smile. He stepped forward and extended a hand to my mother.

"Well, I might not have been around to screen any potential suitors, but if I'm just going by appearances…" she said, looking him up and down. "You fit the part. He's very handsome, Margot," she said as her eyes slid over to meet mine.

Everyone laughed and I shook my head. "I'm glad you approve?" I said, marveling that I was standing here, joking with my mother.

She reached over and took my hand in hers, observing the emerald cut diamond ring on my finger. "Very good, Nathaniel," she said.

He just laughed. "Thank you, Professor Bell."

Mom shook her head at that, but I knew just how

much she loved it. She had been Alderidge's first female professor, after all.

"They're all like us, Mom," I said, moving on. "I trust every one of them."

The spark of momentary joviality instantly left Mom's eyes and was replaced by a haunted one. I could tell, she didn't want to dive into whatever she was about to share. Instead, she walked into the great room and cast her eyes around.

"This is really amazing, Margot," she said, stalling. "I mean, you're not even twenty-one yet, but you're buying oceanfront mansions and renovating. You're starting a school. I…" she shook her head. "I'm so proud of you."

I appreciated the words, but I also wanted to grab her and shake her, force her to tell me what had happened and where she had been.

She walked up to the massive windows that looked out at the ocean and stood there for a few moments with her arms wrapped around herself.

I looked back at my dad. We'd been alone with each other for long enough that I could read him.

That look in Mom's eyes was now in Dad's, to some degree. She'd told him. And it had changed him.

He was married to a mage. He'd never known until I told him. She'd kept her secrets from him, and they'd ripped her away from him for five years.

Half the world blamed him. Thought he did something to her.

But in the end, it had been magic. And we always had to remember the danger magic posed.

"I bought those books at auction," Mom finally said. She stayed there, looking out the window, even though the light was fading. It was a dark haze out there now. "I'd been on the phone all day with the auctioneer. There was someone in Scotland who was trying to outbid me, but in the end, I won the books."

It was Agnes McGregor who had been trying to win them. We'd been to her home on a tiny, isolated island. We'd discussed magic and the locked. She was a cousin, tied to my McGregor blood.

"They took an entire month to arrive," Mom continued. "I stayed busy in the meantime studying the journals I'd found. Piecing together our history, trying to fill in the holes once magic disappeared. But finally, they came. I took them to my office to study them."

I had so many questions I wanted to ask her. About what she knew of magic. About the secret office she'd had above the McCallum room in the library. But right now, I needed to hear this story.

"I'd never seen anything like that sealed book before. But the words on the spine worried me. I set it aside, to investigate at a later time."

She was smarter than us. Nathaniel had read aloud the words without much thought and released Olin, who turned out to be a liar and a wolf in sheep's clothing. And he'd tried to kill me when I found out the truth of who he was.

"But the other," she shook her head. She paused for a long time. And finally, she turned and aimed for a big chair next to the fireplace. She curled up into it, tucking her legs up beneath her. Even though it was the middle of May, she pulled the blanket off the back of the chair and wrapped it around her. "The other was more alluring," she said. Her eyes fixed on the floor, on the big rug, but I knew that it wasn't what she was currently seeing.

Nathaniel reached for my hand as I set off toward the couches. Together, we sat on the one closest to Mom, Dad settling just beside Nathaniel. The others hesitated. I could see in each of their faces that they knew this should be a private conversation between my family members only. But curiosity won out over courtesy. Each of them made their way to a couch or an empty space along the floor.

"I can read, write, speak eight different languages," Mom said. "But my Mandarin isn't the best. I've been working on it but understanding someone speak it and being able to read it are two different games." She shook her head, and I could feel her frustration. "But I could understand just enough to read the first dozen pages. And I was just arrogant enough to believe I could handle the magic."

The very book she spoke of was on the shelf in my office.

"The moment I'd seen it was in Mandarin, my thoughts went to an article I'd just read. It spoke of a small village in a remote part of China. It was far into the mountainous back country. They'd had no contact with anyone other than themselves in centuries."

A cold chill walked along my arms.

My parents were the most curious, knowledge-driven people I'd ever known. Dad read a book a day, and Mom had always been not far behind him.

In the end, her knowledge may have been the reason she was separated from us.

Mom shook her head. "It all happened in a blink. I was thinking about that remote part of China. And I was reading the words in the book. Honestly, I didn't even realize I was saying them aloud. But suddenly these green rings appeared around my hands." She held her hands up, and I knew exactly what she was imagining. I'd seen Olin do this same thing. "And this portal opened." She shook her head again. "I didn't think twice about it. I just stepped into it. One moment, I was standing on the hardwood floor of my office. The next I was on soft jungle soil."

We'd been afraid of the portal book, and this was the reason why.

"I was so excited and elated, and I just wanted to tell someone about it," Mom said, her voice filled with wonder. "But as I turned around, all I saw was more jungle."

She rubbed her hands over her shoulders, and I wondered what she was really seeing.

"I tried to say the words again, to create the portal again. But I could not remember the words exactly." I saw emotions well in her eyes and she shook her head. "Over and over, I said what I thought were the right words. I tried different variations. But no matter what I said, I couldn't remember exactly what was in the book lying on my desk, on the other side of the world."

All this time, I had wondered where my mother might have disappeared to.

China.

She'd been in China.

In the blink of an eye, she'd landed herself on the other side of the globe.

I didn't know what signs of distress I must have been displaying, but Nathaniel gave my hand a comforting squeeze.

"I didn't know what to do," Mom said, the distress climbing in her voice. "So, I just started walking. In my work skirt and shoes, with no jacket, I started walking through that jungle in China."

I squeezed my eyes closed and remembered that first day she didn't come home. Dad and I had gone together back to Alderidge. We'd checked her classroom. Her office. We'd gone to the library. We talked to her friends. We kept expecting to find her asleep at some desk, or in a deep conversation with a student or another professor. My stomach grew sicker the longer we searched the university. We'd gone home well after dark, hoping to find her waiting there, having forgotten to tell us she was running into town, or maybe that she'd had business up in Boston.

But she hadn't been there.

We'd stayed up in the living room all night hoping she would walk through the door.

But she didn't.

And in the morning, Dad finally called the police to tell them his wife was missing.

That's when the investigation started and all the interviews took place, and Dad had to take a leave from work for three weeks.

And every day, Mom didn't come home.

Every day I had to wonder what had happened to her.

"It had to have taken me four weeks to reach the first village," Mom said. "I nearly died of dehydration and a fever. I would have starved to death if not for my magic. But finally, I saw fires down the mountain from me. I stumbled into the village, and thankfully, they did not kill me immediately for trespassing."

I shook my head. This didn't feel real. This was our modern day. Not some movie set a hundred years ago. People didn't get lost and stranded in the jungle. They didn't have to think about starving to death. Or fear that people are going to kill them because they haven't seen an outsider in their entire life.

"It was difficult to communicate with them," Mom said. "As I said, my Mandarin isn't fantastic, but they spoke a different dialect in that village. I could only understand maybe a quarter of what they said, and they could only understand about as much from me. But they were kind. They took care of me. Gave me clothes. Water. Food. A bed to sleep in.

"I tried to explain where I needed to get back to, but they had no idea what America even was. I asked them about airplanes. They'd seen them in the sky but had no idea where they came from. So, I asked about boats. And they told me to keep heading east."

As Mom told her tale, I began to realize just what a miracle it was that she was here in front of me, considering what had happened.

She'd gotten through the jungles of China, to a remote village, and was somehow back here with me.

"They gave me supplies, and I headed out," Mom said. "They had no means of transportation, so all I could do was rely on my own two feet. I spent another few weeks walking through the jungle, hoping I would come across another village to get more supplies and ask for directions."

Mom's expression grew darker. She shifted in her seat, curling tighter in on herself.

"I'd been using my magic to find food and water as I

went," Mom said. "I could only carry so much. There was no one around, so I didn't think twice about it. But one night, I went to sleep. And then I was woken up in the middle of the night by voices and torches. A group of four men grabbed me and dragged me out of my camp and to their village."

My heart was instantly in my throat and I thought I might throw up.

Mom shook her head. "They'd seen me doing magic. Our communication wasn't easy. But they wanted me to do things for them. I didn't know what else I could do but do what they said. I started all their fires. I glamoured their clothes to look more beautiful. I created potions for them that didn't actually work. But…" She let out a shaky breath. "When it was finished, they didn't let me go."

I wanted to grab my mother, to protect her and to comfort her. But I could read every ounce of her body language. The tightness in her entire body. The hard way she was wound into herself, as if she was protecting herself.

"They wouldn't let me leave," Mom said. "No matter how I bargained or pled. The first time I tried to escape, they chained a manacle around my ankle, and I was kept like a dog around a post. They called for me when they needed me. They fed me twice a day. But I was chained to that post for two entire years."

There were varying reactions throughout the room.

Some gasped. Poppy covered her mouth in horror. Peter said something about injustice. The lights in the room flickered with Borden's anger. But I felt a wave of comfort and a rush of ease transferring from Nathaniel, through my hand, and up my arm.

My eyes simply fixed on my mother's ankle, that was poking out from the blanket just barely. There was an angry red scar there.

"One night, the man who kept the keys came into my hut," Mom said. "He was obviously drunk. He was staring at me in a way I didn't like, one that made promises that something was about to change." The temperature in the room seemed to grow colder. "So, I mustered all the strength I had left in me. I grabbed the small table beside me, and I hit him over the head."

It seemed so strange, the fact that Mom hadn't known telekinesis. If she had known it, there were probably a dozen ways she could have made her move. For us, telekinesis was the very first thing we learned. It felt so basic.

But Mom had never known about Nathaniel's book he found in the library.

"I didn't know if he was dead," Mom said, her tone growing a little harder. "I didn't wait around to find out. I took the keys off him and loosed myself. And I just took off into the jungle once more."

I wanted it to be over. I wanted that to be the end.

She got to civilization, caught a flight, and here she was, back home with us.

But there were still two and a half years unaccounted for.

"It took me another month, but I finally made my way to a town. An actual town," I could hear the relief in Mom's voice. "But even though they had roads and stores, and actual civilization, there were no phones anywhere that could make an international phone call. And there was no mail service that could transfer to the states."

So close. She had gotten so close.

"But I talked to a man who could take me by boat to the nearest city with an international airport," she said, sounding hopeful. "I just needed some money. So, I got a job washing dishes and laundry. It would only take me three weeks, and I would have enough."

What I wondered was where did she sleep during those three weeks? Did anyone take her in? Was she homeless?

But this was painful enough for my mother to recount. I wasn't going to drag her into those details.

"I thought I was being careful," Mom said. "I wasn't even sure what I'd done. Or how it was even possible for this to keep happening. But somehow, I exposed myself. A man approached me, tried talking to me about magic, I think. When I refused to talk to him, he threw a bag over my head that smelled strange. And the next thing I knew, I woke up on an airplane."

I could tell Mom was growing tired of sharing this story. Her words grew more wispy. Her tone got quieter.

"I was sold to Kazim Hadad," she said. "And I was taken to his estate in a desert oasis in Sudan. He spoke English quite well, so he could tell me very clearly what he wanted—for me to teach him magic."

My heart hammered harder. This. This didn't even feel human. My mother was sold to someone. Our problems were finding books and trying not to get caught. And she had been sold to someone.

"For two years, I tried. I tried to teach him magic. But no matter what we tried, he was unable to do anything. And he was not very understanding of how little I knew about my own magic. I explained to him that I thought the ability to do magic was hereditary. That it simply wasn't in his blood. He was not an unkind man. But he did not like my answers. So, we continued to try. Day after day."

Not a single one of us interrupted my mother as she told this nightmare of a story. We sat silently, clinging to her every word, an expression of horror on each of our faces.

"I had little way to truly track the time," Mom said. "It felt like it had been a decade since I stepped foot through that portal. But the entire time, I kept trying to remember the words from the portal book. I tried every combination of words I could think of."

A breath hitched in her chest, and I could feel it. The end of this story was approaching.

"One night, as I lay in the bed I'd been given, locked in my room, I said the words," Mom said. "They couldn't have been the correct words, but a portal opened, and I could see a shanty city by the ocean. I took my chances and walked through."

She wiped the corner of her eye on the blanket and pulled it tighter around her shoulders. "I kept picturing our living room, but that wasn't where I landed. I kept getting different cities, all of them ones I'd read about. I went from Sudan to Liberia. From there, I portaled all the way to Venezuela. Then to the Dominican. Three days ago, I made my way to Florida. Then Virginia. And then this afternoon, I walked out into a crowd in front of the Boston Public Library."

That sent my blood cold. How must it have looked? A portal opened, and a ragged woman stepped out into a crowd in a very public place.

"I begged for some money, and caught a taxi home," she said, and her eyes lifted to meet my father's. "And then I was finally home."

"She walked through the door, and I thought surely I had died in my sleep and was being reunited with her," Dad said. There were emotions welling in his eyes as he stared at my mother. I couldn't imagine how this felt.

After all this time, five years, the love of his life had returned.

I squeezed Nathaniel's hand. I loved him more than anything else in this world. I tried to imagine what it would be like for him to simply vanish for five years. I very quickly stopped trying to imagine it.

"And now, here I am," Mom said, her eyes shifting to meet mine. They were filled with tears, but in her face, I saw hope. Despite every nightmare she'd been through in the past five years, I saw hope in her eyes. "And I can't begin to tell you how much I've missed you, Margot."

I got to my feet and crossed to her in an instant. I looped my arms around her, clinging to her like she might disappear again. "Welcome home, Mom."

Everyone in the room stayed silent until I finally released my mother.

"Have you come up with a story yet?" It was Borden who spoke first. All eyes turned to him. "Amelia Bell's disappearance is well known. People are going to wonder what happened to you. Obviously, you can't tell them the truth."

"We'll come up with something," Nathaniel said, giving Borden a dark look for bringing it up in this heavy moment.

Borden just looked at Nathaniel and there was a weighted silence. Borden wasn't wrong. We did need to come up with a plausible story, but tonight wasn't the night for that.

"We should all head to bed," Julie announced. She stood, pulling Marie up after her. "It's late. New semester starts in two days. Peter?" She gave him an obvious look, nodding for him to follow the twins upstairs and give us some privacy. He took the hint and got up to head to bed.

"I think we all better get some sleep," Mary-Beth said, glaring daggers at Borden. He didn't put up a fight. Without another word, he turned and headed for the stairs with her.

But as he passed me, he reached out just one finger, brushing it against the back of my hand. It was a message, a question: *are you okay?*

My eyes rose to meet his. That same question was there in his eyes.

I'm fine, I silently communicated back. I gave a nearly imperceptible nod.

His question answered, he continued to the stairs, followed by Poppy.

And then only my actual family remained. My parents, and my fiancé.

"I'd really love to see your house, Margot," Mom said. And every ounce of her tone told me she was done talking about the past tonight. She was moving into the here and now. "Would you show it to me?"

I nodded and grabbed her hand. Nathaniel held back with my father as we made our way through the house. I showed her the kitchen, my bedroom, then the library.

She'd nearly lost her mind at the rows of shelves filled with hundreds of books, magical and not. And then I showed her the upstairs with its long hallways and endless bedrooms. Finally, I took her up to my office.

"Now this is amazing," Mom said, walking around the room. She took in the windows. "I can't even see anything outside, yet it takes my breath away."

She turned with a smile, and the bookshelves on the back wall came into her view. She let out a breath as a smile formed on her face. "My books."

I turned to face them as well.

In that secret room behind the bookshelves in the McCallum room, there had been a bookcase filled with rare books. They were worth a fortune.

"We had to clean out your secret office," I said. "We didn't dare leave your books there forever. And Dad didn't have a single bit of additional shelf space at home."

"They should be here," Mom said, practically beaming with pride. "Those books are a treasure trove. I can't imagine them in any better place."

"Someday we would all really like to hear the story of that secret office," Dad said teasingly.

Mom smiled and touched his face. "It's really not as grand as you might think," she replied. "But I will tell you. Everything. But not tonight."

Each of us nodded, completely understanding.

We made our way through the rest of the house. I rambled through most of it, telling all the details about the remodel. The contractor. I told her about how Mary-Beth and I picked him, about using the Coin of Compulsion on him. I told Mom how Nathaniel had brought me here before we were together and how I'd said how much I wanted to live here someday.

All of my dreams were coming true.

I had my dream house.

I had Nathaniel by my side, forever.

And now I had my mother back.

"It's all truly incredible," Mom said, doing yet another turn in the living room, taking it all in. "And alchemy." She let out a breathy chuckle. "It's so hard to believe it's real. That's really amazing."

My cheeks actually hurt from smiling so much. I was beaming with pride and appreciation. "Will you help us, Mom?" I asked. "Our new semester starts in two days and Borden's just told us he isn't staying to help teach. We could use your help."

The unspoken truth that she wouldn't be teaching at Alderidge University for a while hung in the air, unsaid.

"Margot, I'm little better than a beginner," Mom said with a sheepish smile. "You've been studying magic to a level I hardly dared dream of. I don't know how much help I could even be."

I took her hands in mine. "More than you know. We need you. And we could use all the help we can get."

Mom offered me a smile, bringing one of her hands

to my cheek. "I'd be thrilled to be one of your students. But I will also help in any way I can."

I pulled her into my arms, embracing her in a tight hug. It felt like it was all pulling together. Finally.

The grandfather clock chimed midnight when I let her go.

"You should get some sleep," I said to her, running my hands up and down her upper arms. "But will you come back in the morning?"

"I will," she said with an enthusiastic nod. "Promise."

She stepped back and grabbed my dad's hand, and my heart swelled at the look he used when he looked at her.

Five years.

Not one had dulled the love between them.

"Goodnight," Nathaniel called to them as they retreated toward the door.

They both called and waved goodnight. And I still couldn't believe my eyes when they walked out, and the door closed behind them.

I just stood there for a solid five seconds staring at the door while I replayed everything in my head that had just happened.

Nathaniel's hands snaked their way around my waist, and he stepped into my view.

"My mom," I said stupidly. I was trying to be in the moment, but I couldn't. I was overwhelmed by places and faces and time. "My mom, here. She's…"

Nathaniel smiled and nodded, pulling me in closer. "She's back, Margot." He leaned his forehead to mine. "You believed and she's back. And it was exactly what you always thought."

It was. I'd suspected her disappearance had something to do with magic, and it did. As soon as we'd learned of the portal book, I thought that was it. And it was.

"I can't believe it," I said, shaking my head. "Everything she's been through. I don't know how she isn't completely mentally broken. How she is even alive. She…" My words trailed off and emotions bit at the back of my eyes. "She was *sold* to someone. She was kept as a prisoner, for years."

Nathaniel reached a hand up and brushed his thumb over my cheek. "But she's here now. Safe and sound. She's with your father. And with us. And we're never going to let anything happen to her again."

Finally, my eyes focused on Nathaniel's. I searched their green depths, and I marveled at him for a moment.

Nathaniel had never even known his own mother. She'd neglected and abused him and then left him when he was only three years old. He'd never seen her since then.

He'd never known a mother.

But here he was, promising to protect my own, and he didn't even know her.

"I love you," I said. And I meant every word, from the tip of my toes to the strand of every hair on my head.

Nathaniel leaned down and gently pressed his lips to mine. "I love you, Margot."

I let out a sigh as the last bits of energy I had escaped my body. It was late. Far later than I ever normally stayed up.

"Take me to bed," I said without a hint of sexual suggestion.

Nathaniel kissed me on the forehead again, and then took my hand and led me toward the bedroom.

We each changed into pajamas and brushed our teeth. And then we climbed up into that massive bed with ten pillows. Nathaniel curled up behind me, wrapping a strong arm around my waist. He pressed a kiss to the back of my neck, and I allowed my mind to turn off into the abyss of sleep.

CHAPTER TWO

The ceiling above me was blinding white when I woke. The sun was streaming in through the curtains pulled over the windows. It was one of those magic moments when I was perfectly comfortable, and the bed was absolutely the right temperature.

I rolled over, and there was Nathaniel, sleeping right beside me.

It wasn't something we'd really talked about. Him moving right into my bedroom, even though we weren't actually married yet. We hadn't had sex yet, even. We were both a little old fashioned in some ways. Yet we were living together in a way that wouldn't change one single bit once we were married.

And that was perfectly okay with me. Because it meant I got to enjoy mornings like this, right now.

He lay there, perfectly at peace. His dark blonde hair

was extra curly right now, full on bed head. His lashes fanned out over his cheeks. His mouth was open just a tiny bit and he breathed softly.

I literally couldn't imagine things any other way. I'd known it from very early on in our relationship that Nathaniel and I would end up together. He was bound to be my husband and I his wife from the beginning. As if we were designed in some pre-existence to be one another's other half.

I scooted closer in the bed and reached across to lay my hand on his chest. He wore a white t-shirt and his boxers, on display since he'd kicked off the blankets.

I smiled as he slowly blinked open his eyes, immediately meeting mine. He reached up a hand, covering mine with his own. I pulled forward with my elbows and kissed him.

It was like a miracle. Just last week, we didn't know where we stood, just that we loved each other like crazy. But we were letting old problems stand in the way of moving forward. And now here we were. Living together. Getting ready to seal our futures together for the rest of time.

"I'll never get over this, Margot Bell," Nathaniel said, whispering the words against my lips. "Waking up beside you every morning. Being able to reach across the bed for you every night."

I smiled against his lips. "Don't get too used to calling

me that name. Before long, it will be Margot Nightingale."

Hearing myself say my name blended with his literally sent a wave of goosebumps flying down my arms.

Nathaniel groaned and I saw a hunger spark in his eyes. "Don't say that name out loud again until after the wedding," he said as he rolled over and kneeled above me, his hands braced into the bed on either side of my head. "Or there won't be much more waiting involved."

I giggled in delight and looped my arms behind his head. "Perhaps we should just elope, then."

Nathaniel smiled but shook his head. "Never. You're my princess, Margot Bell. And I'm going to make sure you get the grand princess wedding you deserve."

His words sank straight into my heart, and he turned me into a puddle with just three sentences. "So, when are we thinking?" I asked quietly.

Nathaniel relaxed himself, lying directly on me. He gently propped up his chin on my ribs to look at me. I just smiled, because I loved this. That the hesitation between us was gone. That we were touching. Together. Living our lives.

"I think perhaps your mother should be involved in this conversation," he said. "I believe mothers like to be involved in the planning of their daughter's weddings."

I grinned, my heart swelling that I actually got this privilege. To have my mom help me plan my wedding. "Well, it's May. I imagine we'll need a few months to plan and shop for a dress and all that. How about the end of August? It will be just between semesters for us."

"You think we'll be ready by then?" Nathaniel asked in surprise.

"I could be ready this afternoon, Nathaniel Nightingale," I teased him. "I'd do it right now. You're the one who says we need a princess wedding."

He smiled and shifted forward, pressing a kiss to my lips. "August sounds perfect."

There was suddenly a knock on the door. "Breakfast is getting cold," Mary-Beth's voice called through the heavy wooden doors. "Stop trying to make baby bunnies and come eat. And hurry up. I saw your mom walking up the driveway with your dad."

And suddenly I was a fifteen-year-old girl again as I sprang from the bed instantly, determined not to get caught in bed with a boy.

Nathaniel's reaction was exactly the same.

I pulled my hair up and out of my face and straightened my pajamas. I was wearing a pair of stretchy, loose fitting white pants and a pale pink top. I didn't have time to hurry and get ready.

Nathaniel pulled on a pair of actual sleeping pants, and we both stepped out of our bedroom, just as there was a knock on the door.

I darted to it and pulled it open.

Like the miracle that she was, my mother stood there. She looked refreshed and clean and human again.

Her hair was washed and curled. She wore clothes that suited her. She didn't look half as tired as she did yesterday.

"You never have to knock, Mom," I said as I immediately stepped forward and hugged her. "You can walk right in whenever you want."

"It felt a little weird doing it," she confessed as I released her and waved her inside. "With so many other people living here, it just seemed polite, I guess."

"You're Amelia Bell," Mary-Beth said from where she stood, leaning against the wall of the entryway. "You're pretty much queen to us. You can go wherever you like, whenever you like, no questions asked."

"I think I like this one," Mom said with a smile.

"I think I like you too," Mary-Beth said with a wink. "You're just in time for breakfast. Hope you're hungry."

I smiled at Dad as he walked in, as well. His eyes shifted to Nathaniel, who was also still wearing pajamas, and his expression grew a little more serious. "Did we wake you?"

I blushed a little as I glanced over at Nathaniel, who was similarly beet red.

"We just had a late start this morning," Nathaniel said. And only he could ever get away with this when it came to my father. Dad loved Nathaniel almost as much as I did.

Mary-Beth had made bacon and eggs and hash browns, and my mouth was instantly watering. Julie was slicing up a watermelon and I pulled some orange juice out of the refrigerator. Just then, Borden came down the stairs, talking with Marie.

For half a moment, my heart leaped with hope. They would be a good fit. Both confident, self-assured people. Both came from rich families who loved to travel.

But as they came closer, they were literally talking about the weather in France this time of year, and they immediately went separate ways and sat at opposite ends of the table.

So much for that short-lived dream.

"So, your dad told me about the study grant," Mom said as she scooped some eggs onto her plate. "I can't believe I missed it. But you finally got to go to Europe! Tell me all about it!"

I'd had plans for my day. I had three new students who would be arriving tomorrow. I needed to get prepared and go over my lesson plans one more time. And now was truly the time to panic, because with Borden disappearing on me, we were down thirty-three percent, teacher wise.

But all that was out the window. There was nothing I would love to do more than sit at this dining table with my mother, and everyone else I loved, and tell her about Europe. Tell her about our discoveries in the libraries here. About the terrifying vision Mary-Beth and I had in Salem with Mare McGregor. We told her about why Borden and I had been expelled from Alderidge. We told her about Olin and everything he'd done and how we needed to track him down, somehow.

We spent the entire morning at that table. And we weren't finished when it was lunch time, so I kept talking while Nathaniel made everyone sandwiches and cut up some apples.

Mom had questions. So, so many questions. She wanted details and the hard, dark parts too. She had her own insights into things, and she turned on some lightbulbs.

And I knew we could do this with her in the picture now. Now that she was here, I knew we could make this work. The academy. Furthering the discovery of magic.

This was my family's work, and we'd do it together.

Mom and Dad went home just before dinner. I was actually exhausted, feeling like I'd been talking all day long, which I had indeed done. Still in my pajamas just before dinner, I excused myself and took a shower. I changed into a comfortable dress, left my hair to air dry and my face without make up.

I walked out of my bedroom to find the house quiet. Marie and Julie had gone out shopping with Mary-Beth, for new summer wardrobes. I had a feeling Nathaniel was up in the office, preparing for our new students.

But out on the back deck, I could see Borden sitting in a chair, drinking something, looking out at the ocean.

I glanced at the kitchen, not really looking at anything in particular.

I could go about my day. I didn't need to do anything. I could stay in this happy place of contentment about my life.

But even as I looked out at Borden, I could see hazy clouds out on the horizon. They were almost always there.

I crossed the room and let myself out through the door onto the deck.

Borden looked up at me with nonchalance and took another draw of his drink. I settled down into the chair beside him. I folded my legs up beneath me and looked out at the ocean.

"You're still leaving in two days?" I asked.

Borden and I didn't beat around the bush with each other. It was one of those things that made us great together.

"Yes," he answered simply.

"Where is it this time?" I asked. I could feel something rising up inside of me, and it was hot and red.

"Hungary," he answered. And I could just feel it coming off of him. He could feel the emotions coming off of me, and his own readiness was rising.

I nodded. I didn't know anything about Hungary. I didn't know the possible mage history there. But that wasn't what I cared about.

"So, you just throw the plan out the window?" I

asked, keeping my tone even. For now. "We're one day away from the semester starting and you decide to change everything?"

I looked over at Borden, who met my gaze. He stared at me with a dark, even look.

"We need you here," I said. "We're starting this school with only three teachers, and now you're taking that number down to two."

It was building inside of me. I felt angrier. More hurt. I felt betrayed.

Borden just sat there, his expression calm, but complex.

"And I need you when it comes to selling the gold," I pointed out. "It's never going to be the same with Nathaniel. You know how he is about money. You and I, it's a partnership, even if you're not doing the alchemy. And now you're just going to leave?"

I was breathing hard by this point. My hands were gripped hard around the arm rests of my chair.

I heard the sound of thunder out over the ocean.

Borden and I stared at each other and I could feel my heart pounding, because we were having another one of those silent conversations.

Borden knew that he was disappointing me. He felt immeasurably guilty.

But he couldn't stay.

Not with him and me and Nathaniel living under the same roof. Not now that I had a ring on my finger.

He had to get some space somehow.

I was angry with him. I needed him and he was leaving. He was vital to our efforts. I felt betrayed.

But I also understood.

I had a ring on my finger.

We both knew what could have been.

And he had to get some space. From me.

A few rebellious tears rose up in my eyes and I looked sharply away from Borden. He reached across the space between us and took my hand, the one that bore Nathaniel's ring, and he, too, looked out over the ocean.

"You'll always come back, right?" I asked with a quaking, shaking voice. My words came out thick and slightly broken.

"Always," Borden promised.

And together, we sat like that, having silent conversations about how difficult this was, but still supporting one another, no matter the current circumstances.

CHAPTER THREE

I was so nervous, I thought I would throw up.

I'd hardly slept the night before. Nathaniel and I had stayed up late, reviewing the plan over and over. Neither of us felt quite prepared, yet we'd spent so much time getting ready for this.

I was terrified and relieved when morning came, and we both finally got up and got ready for the day. We showered. Dressed. Ate the breakfast Borden prepared.

And at eight-thirty, the door opened and in walked Dorian and John. They'd both agreed to help with this first orientation day. Neither of them lived here at Nightingale Academy. They both had their own lives and their own homes. Our next semester of classes started the next day. But for now, they would help orient the new students.

Mary-Beth had given me a copy of the letter she had

sent to them, all of them students at Alderidge. It explained that something had been discovered in their ancestry, something that granted them an invitation to an exclusive schooling program. If they wanted to learn more about the world beyond their own, they were to report here on this date, and be prepared to move in.

It was far better written than I ever could have done. It was intriguing without giving everything away. It was clear their lives would change. It was alluring and tempting.

And now the day had arrived.

And right at nine o'clock, the exact time the letter had instructed, there was a knock on the door.

I kind of froze. Pacing in the great room, my feet suddenly stuck to the floor. My eyes darted to the door, and I stood there like that, all of my students staring at me and waiting.

Nathaniel, dressed in slacks and a button up white shirt, his usual attire, was functional when I was not. He crossed the room to the entryway. He reached for the doorknob. And he opened it.

Three fresh faces stood there, every one of them around my own age.

"Nathaniel," a young man said in surprise. "You…it was you who sent that letter?"

"Please, come inside," Nathaniel said, greeting him and the two women beside him with a smile.

Nathaniel didn't look surprised to recognize one of

the new students walking through the door. Mary-Beth had given us a roster, I suppose. He had just never mentioned that he knew one of the names. "Yes, my fiancée and I sent the letter."

The young man's eyes flicked over to me. "You're engaged?"

Nathaniel smiled and nodded. "As of a few days ago."

"Congratulations," the man offered as the group walked together inside. "You graduate and kick your life into warp speed? Engaged. You live here?"

"Margot has been renovating it for the past year," Nathaniel offered. "We just moved in a little bit ago."

The man's eyes widened, impressed, and he nodded his head.

"Perhaps introductions are in order," Nathaniel said. "Everyone, this is Thomas Kellerman. We had two classes together this last semester. He'll be a senior this fall. Thomas, this is my fiancée, Margot. And this is Mary-Beth Foster, Borden Stewart." He proceeded to introduce the rest of us sitting in the room.

"So this...this is who sent us those letters?" one of the women spoke up. "I mean, the four of you are nearly legends at this point. Borden left the Society Boys and joined up with you lot. And the Fosters...they practically own half the school."

"Not half," Mary-Beth said dramatically. "Just like... thirty percent."

The woman huffed a disbelieving laugh. "This is..."

She shook her head, a look of disbelief on her face. "Now I truly have no idea what we're doing here."

"Can you maybe introduce yourself?" Nathaniel said. And it was strange. That even though we all had a hand in finding these lost mages, we didn't really know them. I had no idea who they were.

"Abigale Dunham," she said, nodding her chin. She had strawberry blonde hair and high cheek bones that made her look fragile like a porcelain doll. "I'll be a sophomore this fall."

Our eyes shifted to the other young woman. Her dark hair was cut short and blunt at her jaw. She wore pristine clothes and stood nervous and stiff. "Alexandra Meirs," she said simply, not one for many words. "Junior."

"We welcome you all," I said, finally finding my voice. It really was intimidating. I was the same age as Alexandra. Younger than Thomas. Barely older than Abigale. And here Nathaniel and I were. In charge. "Thank you so much for responding to our strange letter."

"I thought maybe it was sent by crazy people," Abigale said, a small smile crooking in the corner of her mouth. "But when it said to come to Asteria House, I got more than a little curious."

"The name has changed," Borden spoke up, and it just made my chest ache all the more. He should be doing all of this with us, in equal measure. He was good at it, in his own way. "Considering the Asteria Family no longer owns it."

"Welcome to the Nightingale Academy," Mary-Beth said with a smile.

Thomas' eyes flicked to Nathaniel's. He knew Nathaniel well enough to know that Nathaniel's last name was Nightingale.

"We've invited you all here because you all have a similarity in your ancestry," Nathaniel said. He folded his hands behind his back, and I couldn't help but admire him. The role of headmaster suited him perfectly. "Something similar in your blood."

Our three new students held on to Nathaniel's every word with rapt attention but also speculation.

"Between 1692 and 1693, nineteen people were killed just thirty miles from here, accused of being witches," Nathaniel said. Goosebumps washed over my arms at the power and confidence in his tone, at the reality of the history he recounted. "Between 1626 and 1631, nearly one thousand were killed in Southern Germany, also accused of being witches. More than three thousand in Switzerland. Sixteen hundred in France. On every continent over the span of a thousand years, countless people were killed because others thought they could do something seemingly impossible."

Nathaniel gave a little wave of his hand. A stack of papers was sitting on the coffee table, and with a rush, the top ten of them rushed about the room in a wave, instantly folding up on themselves. Ten origami shapes hung there suspended, folded into perfect form. A crane, a frog, a star, a fox, and other creatures I'd yet seen him make.

"Murder is never a good thing," Nathaniel said as he sent the papers floating throughout the room while our new students gawked in shock. "But they weren't wrong."

"Those witches killed were our ancestors," I said, thinking of Mare and the horrific vision I'd seen of her hanging. "And they were yours."

Nathaniel pulled his wand out from his pocket. It instantly turned crystalline and glowed blue. He next pulled on a pair of gloves, making the wand appear as a pencil once more. "You're here, because over the past four months, my friends and I have tested every student at Alderidge University for others like us." He walked toward Abigale, holding her gaze. "Do you recall getting a certain pencil for a test that may have changed?"

Instantly her eyes lit up and she stood a little straighter.

With a smile, Nathaniel extended his hand and touched the end of his wand to her shoulder.

It glowed.

"You have magic in your blood," he said as he touched Alexandra, and then Thomas. "All of you. The same as all of us." He walked back to the center of the room and came to stand by my side. He removed his gloves and set them, and his wand, down on the coffee table. He released the origami papers and they flattened back out and fluttered back to land in a stack. "Our kind was nearly hunted into extinction and was forced into absolute hibernation for two and a half centuries. But we've brought it back. We need each other. We need you. And if you're willing, we'd like to show you how to use magic once again."

All three of them burst out into reactions, all at once. Shock and questions. Doubt and intrigue. It was chaos, but the overall tone was that of longing for more.

Magic is intoxicating. Just one little display of it is never enough.

They had questions and we gave all the answers we could. They asked to see more magic, and so we showed them. Not just Nathaniel and I; Borden didn't hesitate in showing them his power over electricity. Julie and Marie put on a display. John was more than willing to show them the skills he'd learned. Dorian hesitantly showed off what he could do.

"This is what Nightingale Academy is about," I said as things began to calm down. "We're learning how to harness magic. Extend our abilities. But it's not just about learning magic." I shook my head. "We're a family here. We have to protect each other. Our kind was killed once before. We have to be careful. Watch each other's backs. It's about love and trust. That is what the Nightingale Academy stands for."

Nathaniel's eyes shifted over to the three of them.

They stood there, their eyes big and their chests swelling with excitement. "So, if this is something you can get on board with, if this is something you can believe in, we invite you to join us. This isn't just a school. It's a home. For all of us."

"So, what do you say?" I asked, my heart surging in my chest.

Abigale looked over at Alexandra, a look of excitement on her face. Alexandra seemed nervous, but I could see the spark in her eyes. She was hooked.

Thomas was looking at Nathaniel differently. Not as the strange guy in school who hung out with an odd assortment of people. But as someone he respected. Someone he could see as an equal or a superior.

"I'm in," Abigale said. "For all of it. Schooling. Living here. I'm ready to give this a go."

Alexandra looked around, taking it all in. The house. The people. "It all still seems crazy. But I can't deny what I just witnessed. I'll join in."

My chest swelled with excitement.

Thomas stepped forward and extended his hand to Nathaniel. And Nathaniel smiled as he took it and shook it.

"How could I not join, after what I just witnessed?" Thomas said.

A smile broke out on my face and I felt tears sting the backs of my eyes.

We were doing it. We were in it. The plan. The dream.

Nightingale Academy was up and running, and with the thirteen of us here, we would continue the resurrection of the magical population.

"Well then, welcome," I said. "How about we show you to your rooms?"

CHAPTER FOUR

I WAS GRATEFUL FOR DISTRACTIONS THE NEXT DAY when Poppy and Borden left.

I loved Poppy. She was one of my very closest friends. But she had always been coming and going.

It stung when Borden left.

It was early in the morning. I was already awake, curled up on the couch with a drink, reading the morning paper. He and Poppy came down the stairs, their bags packed. Poppy was dressed in her uniform. Borden looked professional in his slacks and button-up shirt and tie. He didn't have an actual on-site job, he traded stocks on his own. But he always dressed as if he were going to step into a courtroom at any moment.

I'd watched them silently from the couch as they hustled down the stairs with tired, early morning eyes.

Neither of them noticed me, so I stayed silent and still, watching them.

Borden's shoulders were always tight. There was always seriousness in his eyes.

But just before he walked out the door, it seemed to lift, just a little.

I hated that being around me hurt him. I hated that being around me was difficult.

So, in that moment, I told myself to be happy for him.

I got up off the couch and went to prepare for my day.

The first week of our first semester went by in a blink.

Alexandra, Abigale, and Thomas moved into the house. And for the first twenty-four hours it was chaotic and a little stressful as we readjusted to life in the house with two family members gone and three new ones.

But just the very next day, we completed our first classes, with my mother joining them.

The first semester students came to the great room in the morning. Nathaniel and I taught our first classes. Telekinesis. Healing. Self-defense. Daily applicable magic. And history.

We shared and split some classes.

Nathaniel taught telekinesis. I taught healing. We both taught self-defense and the DAM class. Nathaniel taught history.

It was a wonderful first day, and every one of our

students did great. Our star was clearly going to be Alexandra, who was able to perform everything within a second try. Thomas picked up on everything quickly. And Abigale was too shocked by everything to do it particularly clear or quick. But she managed. Mom was a quick learner, but I was fast realizing that she knew a few things when it came to magic, but it was limited. She had been a full-time professor, as well as a mother and wife. Unlike myself, she hadn't had the opportunity to dedicate herself full time to magic.

We took a break for lunch, and dismissed the first semester students. And just after dinner time, John and Dorian arrived, and they combined with Julie and Marie, our second semester students.

We worked on transfiguration, compulsion, glamouring, assorted magic, and once more, history—part of which included working on their grimoires, a recounting of their own personal history and magical study.

I had to admit, it was more fun working with the second semester students. But I felt more confident in my teaching when it came to the first semester group.

Nathaniel and I both went to bed that night utterly exhausted, but incredibly satisfied.

And this continued for the next three days.

On the fourth day, Borden returned with Poppy. They hadn't found any new mages, but Borden brought a new magical book he'd found in a library in Hungary.

Nathaniel sent out a request for a translator, and Borden dove right in, helping with the teaching.

The difference in having two teachers and three was immense. The burden was much lighter. The lessons more interesting and intense.

I wished I could count on him being here all of the time. But I had to let him be free.

Saturday night, the phone rang. Abigale answered it and called for me in the kitchen just a moment later.

I took it from her and held it to my ear.

"Come over for dinner tomorrow," Dad's voice came through the phone. In the background, I could hear my mother humming, miraculous and clear. "I want to hear all about your first week at the school."

I'd agreed with a smile. "And bring Nathaniel, of course."

So, Sunday afternoon, Nathaniel and I stepped out the front door. Hand in hand, we set off down the sidewalk, bound for my parents' home.

"You know," Nathaniel said as we walked. "Sometimes I miss you living with your father. There's just something about the possibility of being caught. The danger is not quite the same living on our own."

I looked over at him with an open-mouthed gasp. "Nathaniel Nightingale. You're such a rake!"

He pulled me to him, his hand clutching my hip as he tipped my lips up to his. My hand rose to lace in his hair, and I smiled, utterly thrilled and happy in this moment.

"I have to admit," I said as we continued on our way. "I replay that night over and over in my head. The night you climbed in through my bedroom window and practically shoved me into my bed. Your lips were so desperate that night."

"They're desperate every moment I look at you, Margot," he said, once more stopping me right in the middle of the sidewalk and tipping my face up so he could show me how much he meant the words.

"I'm not sure how I'm supposed to feel," a voice called. I whipped up to find Mom two houses down. She was kneeling in the front gardens, pulling weeds. "On the one hand, that's my daughter you're kissing like she's the last bit of oxygen on Earth. On the other, I've never seen anyone look at her the way you do, Nathaniel."

Nathaniel flushed beet red and sheepishly continued walking beside me. "Sorry, Professor Bell. Margot just seems to awaken a new man in me."

She gave him this smug little smile as she stood and pulled off her gardening gloves. "Professor Bell. You really need to stop flattering me."

Nathaniel smiled, and heat filled my entire core with it. It was often so rare, but it was one of the most beautiful things I'd ever seen.

"Sorry," he said. "Habit. Four years of university, and

it's kind of drilled into me to call every adult older than me Professor."

"Well, I might not be old enough for you to call me Mom," she said as she turned for the stairs. "But you can certainly call me Amelia."

"I'll try," Nathaniel said as we followed her up the stairs. "But old habits die hard."

Mom just chuckled and stepped inside.

It smelled great. In the years that Mom wasn't around, I'd taken the mantle of cooking the majority of meals. Dad was a bit of a fool in the kitchen. But with Mom home, it once more smelled like my childhood.

I found Dad setting the table. He looked up from his book to us with a smile. "Well hello, you two love birds."

"Arthur," Nathaniel said, smiling as he crossed to my father and wrapped him in a quick hug. "Can I help?"

"Cups, please," Dad instructed.

"I think I missed something," Mom said as she leaned over to me and whispered. "I never knew your father had a son."

I laughed and leaned in to hug her from the side, watching as our men finished setting the table. We grabbed the food from the oven and stove and set it on the table. Together, we settled around it and served our dishes up.

"So," Mom said. "How was it? Your first week of being teachers?"

I smiled, swallowing my bite of food. "It was pretty

incredible," I said, looking over at Nathaniel. "I always knew I wanted to be a teacher, but teaching magic certainly beats teaching Latin."

"I always knew you would be a natural," Mom said with a smile.

My parents had questions though, about the academy. And I wouldn't have expected anything less from a couple of professors. They wanted to know about our curriculum and how we handled grades. They wanted to know about tests and midterms. They asked about the students and recruitment.

My chest swelled with pride as we answered their questions. We weren't typical like a normal school. There were no grades given, they either mastered certain aspects of magic, or kept trying. There were no tests until they had to do something in the real world. And graduation was when we couldn't teach them any more basics.

But we'd created something exceptionally special.

"I still can't believe it," Mom says, shaking her head. "You're only twenty and twenty-three. When I was your ages, I hadn't even met your father yet, and all I could handle was studying and student teaching. You two have gone and accelerated everything and are handling it like you've been doing this for years."

I smiled at her compliments, but inside, I felt my heart break a little bit. Because part of the reason why I could do what I was doing at my age was because of her disappearance when I was still so young. I'd been forced to grow up a lot faster.

And Nathaniel. Nathaniel had every single event in his life forcing him to grow up faster than he should have.

"You've raised quite the impressive daughter," Nathaniel complimented my mother. He looked over at me and took my hand, looking at me with so much admiration I thought I would melt.

"Have you two set a date yet?" Mom asked. "That sounds like something I should be panicking and stressing over. Planning a wedding."

I laughed, meeting her eyes. "We're talking the end of August. Just before the semester starts."

"Thank Hera for that," Dad said with a raise of his glass.

"Three months," Mom calculated. "That's plenty of time!"

I laughed, because only my mother would think that was more than enough time. She was so simple and straight forward when it came to everything.

"How about we go wedding dress shopping this weekend?" she asked as she cut into her pot roast. "And we can take care of flowers the week after that. Do you have a venue picked yet?"

Nathaniel and I glanced at each other. "We're just going to do it at the house. A small ceremony with friends and family."

"When do we get to meet your parents, Nathaniel?" Mom asked, casual and completely unknowing. "Where do they live?"

My stomach knotted and my palms went a little cold. I choked on the bite I was trying to swallow.

"Amelia," Dad started to say, laying his hand on hers, ready to try and diffuse the awkward situation Mom had unknowingly walked into.

"No, it's okay, Arthur," Nathaniel said. He wiped his mouth with his napkin. He sat a little straighter and met my mother's eyes. "I was actually taken from my parents' custody when I was three years old," he explained, so calm and accepting of it, despite the darkness of its reality. I watched as my mother's expression paled. "They had multiple substance abuse issues. They couldn't take care of me and my two older siblings."

My eyes fell to the table. It wasn't fair. Why were some children so unlucky to be born into families who just couldn't provide the safe environment every single child deserved?

"We were split up," Nathaniel continued. "Placed into foster care. And that's where I stayed until I turned eighteen. Getting the opportunity to attend Alderidge University was…" Nathaniel shook his head. I knew just how much he was underselling this right now. He'd had to drag himself through hell to get there. Two years in juvenile detention. Multiple expulsions from his high school. And then a complete turnaround of his life when he realized the path he was headed down would lead him straight to jail or death. "It meant everything to me. But to answer your question, I'm afraid you won't ever be meeting them. I haven't known where they were since I was three."

Mom set down her utensils and looked at Nathaniel with compassion and pity. "Oh, Nathaniel," she said in a slow breath. "I am so sorry. That… No child should ever have to go through all of that."

Nathaniel drew in one breath and shook his head. "It's okay. It wasn't an easy path. But our trials make us grow as people. I suppose I'm grateful for all the experiences I've gone through. They've led me right to where I am today. And I couldn't be more grateful for that."

I reached over and took Nathaniel's hand in mine.

This. This was why I worked so hard and pushed through everything. Because after everything he'd been through, Nathaniel deserved a beautiful life from here on out.

"I know I said I wasn't old enough," Mom said as she reached across the table and grabbed Nathaniel's other hand. "But every person deserves to have someone to call Mom. I'm honored to have you as part of our family, Nathaniel."

It was a perfect night. We ate dinner together. And then Nathaniel and my father ended up in the living room, talking about history and books. Mom and I went up to her bedroom and worked on wedding plans, listing out everything that needed to be done to get ready.

I didn't want anything fancy. I wasn't one for big events. But I knew Nathaniel wanted me to have something special. So we talked about flowers. We talked about pictures. Announcements. A trip to go buy Nathaniel's wedding band.

We listed out all the little details we needed to take care of and assigned them timeframes.

This was my dream. Sitting in my parents' home, with both of them present. Being a woman planning her wedding with her mother, listening to her fiancé and father laughing and joking about the ridiculousness of Napoleon Bonaparte.

What more could I ask for?

But then it was all ruined when later that evening, Nathaniel's voice called for me from downstairs.

I came down in a hurry, alarmed by his tone.

Together, he and Dad were hunched over the Sunday morning paper, both their eyes glued to a headline.

My stomach was twisted in knots before I even leaned over Nathaniel's shoulder to read what it said.

Lee Wickham found dead in home. Suspended in air, frozen. No explanation.

Quickly, my eyes read through the article. This Lee Wickham was a leader in England. His wife had been out of town and found him when she arrived home. There, she'd found him suspended in the air, as if floating. There was a black ring around his neck, and his skin was frozen to the touch.

"It's Olin," I said. My eyes flicked up to Nathaniel's at the same moment my hand rose up to touch my throat. "That's exactly what he'd tried doing to me that night. I'd never felt cold like that before. I have no doubt it could have killed me if he'd kept a grip for a few more moments."

Nathaniel nodded in agreement. "He was always talking about going after political leaders. He wanted to demand rights for mages. If Lee Wickham disagreed with him…"

I shook my head as Nathaniel trailed off.

"This is the same man who came after you?" Mom asked, her tone growing harder.

I nodded. "I have no doubt. It's the same thing he did to me. It fits, talking to a political leader. It has to be Olin Rayburn."

"What can be done then?" Dad asked. The look in his eyes was frightened but dark. He knew what had happened to me at Olin's hands.

I looked back at Nathaniel. "We need to talk to the others. But this is a start. We at least know he's been in England. Recently."

Nathaniel nodded and we both stood.

"We'll handle this," I said, looking at my parents. "I don't want either of you feeling as if you need to do anything. This is our fight."

"Margot-" Mom started to protest.

But I raised a hand, cutting her off. "We'll handle it. Thank you for dinner tonight."

And without another word, I grabbed Nathaniel's hand, and pulled him out the door and into the dark night.

We talked on our way home. We debated. We ran through possibilities.

But this was entirely new territory. We weren't trackers. We'd never fought in any wars.

This was something that had to be handled collectively.

We were lucky, because Dorian and John happened to be at the house when we arrived.

"Guys, we have a lead," I said the second I walked into the living room where everyone was gathered.

We called everyone into the great room and then Nathaniel showed everyone the newspaper article.

"It has to be Olin," Mary-Beth blurted out, instant fire in her tone. "Margot, that's exactly what he did to you."

I nodded. "I don't doubt it was him. I mean, we saw that tiny glimpse when he walked through the portal. It easily could have been somewhere in England. It's where he's from. It's where he tried to initiate change before."

"It was ignorant of us to not automatically check there first," Borden said. Outside, I heard the clap of distant thunder.

I had to agree with him. We truly should have assumed that was where he would go first.

"I'm scheduled to go to England next," Poppy said. "I'll be there for six days instead of my usual four."

"I'm going with you," Borden stated, even though that was the plan anyway. "And I'm staying for however long it takes to find Olin."

"I'll go with you," John said, sitting forward just a bit. "I don't like the idea of him just waiting out there in the wind."

"We have to be smart about this," Nathaniel said as he sat on the arm of one of the couches. "England might be a lot smaller than the United States, but it's still an entire country. We could spend the rest of our lives searching for him."

I stood straighter. "What if we were able to create some kind of tracking spell?" I said, my eyes widening.

"Is that something you know how to do?" Abigale asked, intent interest in her eyes.

I shook my head. "No. I haven't seen anything about that in any of our books. But we've created our own kind of magic before. Why couldn't we do it again?"

Borden stood, looking ready to head off right this very instant. "It's settled then. Poppy, John, and I will go to England and take care of Olin. The rest of you, stay here and help Margot create a tracking spell."

"I'm not staying here," I said, glaring at Borden with surprise.

Borden shook his head. "Look around, Margot. We have veritable children on our hands." That brought a few mumbles of outcry from the students. "They're likely to get themselves killed. We need this school, and we need all of them to get stronger and more knowledgeable. You and Nathaniel have to stay here. You can work on that spell and let us know when you've perfected it."

"I don't like it," I said, shaking my head, even though a stone of realization was sinking in my stomach. Borden was right. Even Poppy and John were at terrible risk going with Borden. They had only finished one semester of training.

"We'll be working on every bit of self-defense magic I know," Borden said, his tone shifting to reassuring. "We'll be studying every bit of tactical magic we can in the meantime while we track him."

I didn't like it. But I didn't know what else could be done.

CHAPTER FIVE

It was chaos the next morning. Borden, Poppy, and John got all packed. Who knew how long they would be gone. So, they had heavier suitcases than normal. I wanted to argue all the way to the airport, but I just kept thinking about Peter and Alexandra and Abigale and Thomas. They had one week of training. They knew almost nothing.

I couldn't abandon them. Yet, in the same breath, I felt like I was abandoning the other three in sending them to England after Olin on their own.

I was nearly in tears when I hugged the three of them goodbye at the airport. My guilt was eating me alive. But they simply rushed off, in a hurry to catch their flight.

By the time we arrived back home, classes were about to begin. We were all distracted as we worked on telekinesis. No one had their heart in it as Nathaniel went over history.

So, it was a relief when noon came around and classes for first semester students were over.

Nathaniel and I retreated upstairs with Mary-Beth, Julie, and Marie to my office.

"How many translations have we gotten back?" Mary-Beth asked as she started pulling books off the shelf.

"Two of the Swiss ones," Nathaniel reported as he grabbed the very manuscripts from a shelf and set them on my desk in the center of the room. "Three of the German ones." He set those down as well.

We scoured the library. All of our bedrooms. And for the next five hours, we poured through the books and manuscripts, searching all the words for…anything. Any clues. And when Dorian showed up just after five for his classes, we decided to skip them for the day.

This was more pressing and more important.

I shook my head. "This is so frustrating. Because this should have been so much more applicable back in the day. Tracking was a specific job. There has to be some kind of record of this type of spell. But it could be in any of those books sitting with the translators."

"What's the schedule?" Mary-Beth asked without looking up from the book she was pouring over.

"Translation is slow work," Nathaniel said as he scanned through one of the German translations. "We've been getting about one a week, from each language. We really can't hope for faster than that or we might be getting all kinds of mistakes that could put us in danger."

"We need a magical translation spell," Marie said. She was thumbing through yet another book.

"That would be a miracle," Nathaniel said, and I could just imagine him drooling over some kind of translation spell that could instantly change the words.

We started taking notes. Mary-Beth transcribed any small possibilities and we had tabs and strips of paper bookmarking different tomes. We spouted off ideas and possibilities.

The hour showed midnight when each of our eyes were exhausted and straining in the low light.

"It's a good start," I said, nodding. "I don't think we're going to make any sense of this tonight. And I'm not sure we're quite there. Let's sleep on it until morning."

And so, each of us completely exhausted, we headed down the spiral staircase. They all disbursed down the hall, and Nathaniel and I said goodnight to Dorian as he walked out.

Together, we headed into our bedroom. We brushed our teeth and, tired beyond belief, collapsed into bed.

Nathaniel reached across and pulled me in against his chest. "I have to admit, even though today was stressful and I feel the clock ticking, I loved every second of what we did today."

I smiled in the dark and rolled back over to him. "I kind of loved it too. I think this is one of my favorite parts. Creating our own magic. Everything is so often about the past for us. It's kind of refreshing doing our own thing."

I felt Nathaniel nod in agreement. "There's a lot at stake. So…I feel…guilty. Because I'm happy, Margot Bell. I love this life we've created."

I smiled in agreement. Softly, I tipped my head back to him, and my lips found his in the dark.

I couldn't agree more.

We received a call from Borden the next morning. He'd arrived in the area where Lee Wickham was murdered and had managed to get himself an appointment with the head investigator later that evening. In the meantime, he and John were checking the area themselves for any signs of Olin's whereabouts. He'd give us another call that night if he found anything, otherwise he would call again the next morning.

So we went about our day. We taught the first semester students. We had lunch. And we had actual class with the second semester students. Only after dinner did we all go to the office again and search through more books.

We had a few leads. But they weren't particularly

solid. I had a feeling that we would indeed be creating a tracking spell on our own.

We could throw something together and force it immediately. But as we had learned, we had to be careful. Magic was serious, dangerous business. We didn't need anything going massively wrong.

We didn't get a call from Borden that night, and my heart sank into my stomach.

Neither Nathaniel nor I said much as we crawled into bed that night. I stared at the ceiling, letting everything tumble around in my head. The spell. The fact that Olin was out there, what he wanted to accomplish. It was finally sinking in that he'd actually murdered someone. That he'd tried to kill me.

My world was growing more dangerous by the day.

In the morning, the phone rang, and I practically ran to where it sat on an end table beside the couch.

"The investigator met with us this morning," Borden said, not bothering with a second of pleasantries. "They have no idea what could have caused the chancellor's death. They can't explain the levitation."

"Did you alter his memory of it?" I asked. I held the phone slightly away from my ear and Nathaniel leaned in close, attempting to hear the conversation as well.

"No," Borden said, letting out a hard breath. "What's the point? It's been all over the news. Too many people know now. There were plenty of people investigating the scene."

He was right. It had gone too far to consider taking anyone's memories of what they'd seen.

"Any leads on Olin?" Nathaniel asked.

"They've canvased the area and talked to every neighbor within a five-kilometer radius," Borden said. "No one has seen anything. They haven't found anything that makes them think they're going to catch whoever did this."

"He probably just teleported away," I said, feeling sick. "Why would he stick around? Why risk being seen? He could open a portal, standing right over the man's body, and go anywhere in the world."

"Exactly," Borden said. "Olin could be anywhere. The fact that he went straight to his homeland of England says something, so I'm holding on to the hope that he'll stay in this country. He doesn't speak any other languages. He isn't familiar with any other territory. If he thinks he understands the government here in the slightest, I hope he'll stick with what's somewhat familiar."

"Let's hope," I said. "In the meantime, we're working on creating a tracking spell, but it might be a week or so until it's testable."

"Do what you can," Borden said. "But be safe. I'll call again tomorrow morning with another update."

We said our goodbyes and ended the call.

How long was it going to go on like this? This feeling of unsettledness, having no idea how long it would be until we found Olin. And even when he was found, would we really be able to destroy him?

"What are the ethics in this?" Alexandra asked from behind. We both turned and saw her standing in the kitchen. "I assume that was an update on Olin. What's the ethical choice in taking care of a man who has his own opinions that differ from your own? He's a danger, but does he deserve to die?"

Her words tied my insides up in knots. Because she wasn't wrong. I had nearly died at Olin's hands once, so to me, it was very simple. Black and white. But I wasn't omniscient. I wasn't the queen of anything.

"This sounds like a great discussion topic in our history class today," Nathaniel said, smooth and easy.

We did have a great discussion in history. We shared the full story of Olin, his involvement with Sandris. And then our own experience with him. We shared every detail, including the lies he'd told us, how he tried to manipulate the second-semester students. We told them everything, in as unbiased a way as we could manage.

We'd debated. But in the end, it really wasn't much of a debate.

They all agreed. Olin was dangerous. He put us all in danger. He had to be stopped. Permanently.

Immediately after our discussion, we moved on to self-defense magic, mingled with basic fighting tactics.

It was the most engaged they'd yet been in a lesson.

The next morning, we got another phone call from Borden. He had no new news.

We taught. We studied books for possibilities to use in our tracking spell.

We went to bed.

Repeat.

In the morning, I rolled over as Nathaniel reached for me. I scooted closer, burrowing myself into his chest. I relished in the warmth as his arms wrapped around me, appreciating their strength, and even more appreciating his bare skin. It had been a hot night and neither of us were wearing many clothes.

How we'd not yet had sex was a mystery.

"I'm taking you out tonight," Nathaniel said softly into my hair. "We've done nothing but work for so long. We're going on a date."

"Oh, yeah?" I asked, smiling sleepily. "I like this idea."

So, I'd spent some time doing my hair. I got dressed in a cute summer dress. I'd splashed on some perfume. And then we had a normal day. We taught the first semester. We taught the second semester. And then when we were done at five o'clock, we walked out the door.

"I think we need to go car shopping this weekend," Nathaniel announced as we walked down the sidewalk, hand in hand. "We're not going to be able to get along without one for much longer."

"I think you're right," I said. I honestly didn't love

driving, and I was actually content walking everywhere. But it wasn't always going to cut it. We would need to travel. And we could only carry so many grocery bags. Plus, summer wouldn't last. "We'll head to the dealership this weekend."

Nathaniel nodded in agreement, and it was decided.

"So where are you taking me?" I asked, looking up at Nathaniel's face as I cuddled myself close into his side.

"I thought we'd enjoy a dinner out," he said, smiling down at me. "And then I have a few surprises after that."

I smiled, because I loved that idea. Nathaniel and surprises were my favorite combination.

We ended up at a sweet little clam shop. We laughed and talked about normal, everyday things. We ignored the pending doom over our heads that was Olin. We didn't talk about magic even once.

When we were finished, Nathaniel tugged me down the sidewalk, and I happily and blindly followed him.

I didn't expect him to direct me to Alderidge. A flood of familiarity washed through me as we walked through the gates and stepped out onto the grounds.

It was quiet considering it was summer. There wasn't a single student milling around. No one rushing to get to class. Just a single, solitary grounds keeper off in the distance, mowing the lawn.

"Come on," Nathaniel said, looking back at me, and pulling me toward the north side.

Instantly, I knew where we were going.

We cut straight to the stone fence that ran north from the university. We walked to and through the gate that had the warning sign on it. The garden was more wild than normal, not having been visited in weeks. The side of the building looked further decayed from the last time we were here. A storm and then a fire destroyed it decades ago, and for whatever reason, the university chose not to put any money into fixing it.

We walked through the abandoned garden, and then, there it was.

Nathaniel's solarium.

The door felt familiar and warm as we turned the handle and stepped inside. Instantly, the scent of Nathaniel flooded my nose, even though it had been weeks since he had moved out.

"It's sad seeing it empty," I said, walking to the middle of the brick floor and looking around. "I always loved this space."

Nathaniel didn't look around though. His eyes were fully fixed on me, and I blushed at the way they ran up and down me, taking every bit of me in.

"Thor's hammer, you're beautiful, Margot," he said, and his words sounded absolutely reverent. Slowly, he walked toward me, and I raised my chin, feeling heat creep up my entire body.

His hands came to my hips and I brought my own to the back of his neck.

"It's been a long time since we've actually been alone," I said in a husky voice.

"It has," he said in agreement.

Slowly, gently, I raised my mouth to his. And softly, he lowered his lips to mine.

Nathaniel's hands gripped my dress at my hips possessively. I leaned into him, my chest pressing against his. I let my mouth open to greet his tongue and he granted me my wish immediately.

He turned me and backed us into the brick wall. The heat in my body grew more frantic, and maybe Nathaniel felt the same way, because he gripped me at my hips and hoisted me until my legs were wrapped around his waist. He pinned me against the brick with his hips pressed into mine and I moaned at the ecstasy of it.

I tilted my head back and Nathaniel's lips trailed from mine down my jaw. His hand rose to my neck, running up the side of it, bracing me there as he pressed hot kisses to the side of it. My hands slid into his hair and my entire body went slack and languid with desire.

"Let's just go to City Hall right now," I panted, nearly delirious. "I'm ready now, Nathaniel. Make me your wife right now."

He looked up at me, his lips swollen and wet. "Your mother and all of our friends would kill us if we skipped the wedding."

"Good thing we're mages and can heal each other," I

said, too hungry to wait for anymore words. I brought his lips back to mine.

I meant it. If he would, I would go with Nathaniel to City Hall right then and sign the papers before a judge. But I also didn't mean it. I was enjoying the journey to becoming husband and wife. I was living in this hot moment, stolen on the grounds of the university that kicked me out.

I pushed off from the wall and Nathaniel set me back on my feet. It wasn't enough though. I pushed Nathaniel down, till he was sitting on the brick floor. Without hesitation, I settled into his lap, one knee on either side of his hips.

His hands rose up, tangling into my hair as again, he brought my lips to his. I sighed into his mouth as he tipped backward until he was lying flat on his back.

I didn't know how long it took until we noticed. But suddenly I was aware of every bit of dirt, floating in the air. All the broken twigs and loose flower pedals outside the solarium were floating in the air. And there was this golden shimmer around the both of us.

I sat back, looking down at Nathaniel. His hair was now a wild mess. His lips were swollen, and there was this wild, savage look in his eyes.

But he was mine. And he had claimed me.

"I love you, Nathaniel Nightingale," I declared, no hesitation. "And I cannot wait to be your wife."

. . .

The next morning, I woke up early. I was careful not to wake Nathaniel. I climbed out of bed, dressed, and silently slipped out of the house. It was a fifteen-minute walk. I met with the seller, I handed over the money. I stopped for supplies on the way home. And then I headed back.

I was grinning ear to ear. I'd been waiting four weeks for this.

As I walked through the gate, I struggled to balance the box, but kept my grip. I walked through the front doors to find the house still quiet. Apparently, this Saturday was for sleeping.

I left the box on the floor in the living room and slipped into my bedroom.

Nathaniel was still sleeping. His dark blonde hair was wild. He was so sound asleep, his mouth was partly open. He slept like the dead.

I crawled up onto the bed, and slowly, I slipped my hands beneath his shirt and ran my hands up and over his stomach, then his chest.

That woke him instantly, with wide, surprised eyes, he caught my face.

"Well, if that isn't a good morning, I don't know what is," he said groggily, a smirk forming on his lips.

"Wake up," I said as I shifted forward and pressed a quick kiss to his lips. "I have a surprise for you."

He cocked an eyebrow at that and watched me climb

off the bed. He climbed out after me, and followed me out into the living room.

With a manic, very pleased grin, I walked to stand beside the box and looked down at it. "Open it," I said with enthusiasm, glancing back at Nathaniel.

He cast me a wary look but stepped forward. Cautiously, he took the corners of the box, and opened them.

Instantly, a head sprang out, followed by two big paws on the edge of the box.

Nathaniel looked up at me with awe in his eyes.

"You got me a dog," he said, his voice full of wonder and elation.

I nodded excitedly. "Well, technically he's still a puppy, but one day, he will be a dog."

With a huge grin, Nathaniel hooked his hands beneath the puppy's front legs and lifted him from the box. His sleek black body was shiny and healthy. And already huge considering he was less than three months old.

"He's beautiful," Nathaniel declared as he cuddled the beast into his chest. "Is this a Great Dane?"

I nodded with a smile. "You said you wanted a huge dog. The breeders said the dad is over two hundred pounds and the mom is about one sixty."

Nathaniel chuckled as he wiggled his fingers in front of the puppy, who nipped at them playfully. "He's going to get bigger than I am, Margot."

I laughed. The puppy wiggled and kicked his legs, biting at Nathaniel's ear. Nathaniel set him down, and the puppy immediately dipped into a play bow, then jumped around and let out a bark.

"What the hell is going on down there?" Mary-Beth called grumpily as she came down the stairs on groggy legs. Her eyes widened as the puppy ran over to her, licked her toes, and then ran off, running up and down the space between the living room and kitchen.

With wild confusion, she looked up at me. "That's a Great Dane, Margot," she said. "Do you have any idea how much it's going to slobber and how big its poops are going be?"

I just shook my head and rolled my eyes. "It's just a puppy. Besides, it's Nathaniel's dog now. He'll be the one taking care of the gross stuff."

"Oh, thanks, my love," Nathaniel chuckled.

Just then, Marie and Julie came down the stairs and immediately started shrieking in delight when they saw the puppy.

"What will you name him?" I asked Nathaniel as I wrapped my arms around his waist and leaned into him. We watched as Julie ran up and down the living room with our new family member.

Nathaniel paused for a moment, contemplating. "Hmm… I think Khan is fitting."

I gave him a look of doubt. "As in Genghis?"

The look on his face told me Nathaniel knew he was

being ridiculous. He pressed his lips together and nodded. "He may be notorious as the biggest warlord in history, but what he accomplished is massive. The man conquered more territory than any other in history. Nearly five million square miles."

"You want to name your dog after a blood thirsty war lord?" I asked doubtfully.

Nathaniel extended his hand, indicating the puppy, who ran and jumped at Marie. He already came up to her waist. "Are you trying to tell me the name doesn't fit?"

I had to admit, Khan did fit the shiny black great Dane. "You history nerd," I teased him, shaking my head, even as I snuggled up into him.

The phone rang and I walked over to pick it up. "Good morning, Borden," I said without waiting to hear if it was actually him.

"You sound in a good mood," he noted immediately.

"It's a beautiful morning," I said. I really was in a good mood.

He made a grunting sound. "We haven't found any more leads," he said, getting to the point of his call. "The trail is cold, and I don't think anything is going to change. We're just wasting time here looking around for a ghost."

Immediately, my good mood was gone. "What are you saying?"

"I'm saying that we're coming home," Borden said. "We aren't going to get anything else accomplished like this, so we're all coming home. We'll help you get that tracking spell figured out."

It kind of felt like a punch to the gut. Like Borden didn't think we could do this on our own, so he was going to have to come back and take care of it himself.

"Borden, we-"

"That's not how I meant it, Margot," he cut me off. "I know you could manage this on your own, and Nathaniel is perfectly capable, too. I didn't mean it that way. I'm just saying I'll be better use there than here right now."

I nodded, grateful for his change of words. "Alright, when should we pick you up from the airport?" I asked.

"Tomorrow night," he said. "And it won't just be the three of us."

"You found another mage?"

And with my question, every set of eyes in the house snapped to me.

"Yeah," Borden said, and finally, he sounded hopeful. "And he was aware of what he is. He doesn't know much, just how I was before I talked to you and Nathaniel. But he's agreed to come back to the States with us and join the academy."

"That's wonderful," I said, smiling as I looked around at my friends.

"See you tomorrow night," Borden said, and he ended the call.

CHAPTER SIX

Nathaniel and I went out and bought a car the very next morning. It was sleek and shiny, and it was the biggest one that could hold the most people. We'd both smiled like fools when they handed over the keys and told us congratulations.

It felt…selfish, taking a lazy afternoon and relaxing and enjoying ourselves. But we both needed a reprieve. There was little we could do that particular day, and we were just waiting. So, we'd cruised through town in our new car and then got lunch. Afterwards, we picked up Mom and Dad and took them for a ride, and they'd gushed over the beautiful vehicle.

But like all relaxing things, it came to an end. At six, we headed to the airport.

We waited outside with nervous excitement.

Fifteen minutes later, I got a glimpse of Poppy's red

hair and then her smiling freckled face. She was followed by John, and then Borden, who was followed by a man I didn't recognize.

His skin was dark and his hair black. His eye lashes were so dark it almost looked as if he were wearing eye makeup. He had flawless skin and it stood out in sharp contrast with the stark white tunic he wore.

They all stopped just in front of Nathaniel and me.

"Welcome home," I said, pulling Poppy in for a hug, then John. Hesitantly, I looked at Borden, but in the end, I reached for him as well, holding him tight.

I had worried I would never see them again. I'd never voiced it to any of them, but I knew there was that possibility. Olin had killed before. He was powerful and strong. He could have overpowered them if they'd found him.

But here they were, safe and sound.

I backed away and my eyes turned to the newcomer.

"Margot, Nathaniel, this is Aleem Syed," Borden said, extending a hand toward the newest mage.

"It's a pleasure to meet you," Aleem said. His accent was difficult to distinguish. A mix of middle Eastern and English.

I extended a hand to shake his, but I watched as he very obviously tucked his hands behind his back, and I wondered at the gloves he wore.

But I didn't make a big deal out of it. I dropped my

hand back to my side. "And you as well," I said, smiling warmly. "Welcome to Massachusetts."

"It's a pleasure to finally visit the states," he said with an excited nod.

"Shall we get going?" Nathaniel asked, noting the surge of people around us.

Borden nodded and we waved him toward the car. "Wow, someone finally did it," he said, noting the brand-new car. "Guess it was about time one of us had our own wheels."

"Speak for yourself," John said as he lifted his bag into the trunk. "I bought my first truck when I was sixteen."

"Guess we all know who the real adult is now," Poppy teased as she too deposited her bag.

We all climbed in and Nathaniel cautiously guided us away from the curb and out into the flow of cars driving through the Boston-Logan Airport.

"So, Aleem," Nathaniel said as he watched the road. "Why don't you tell us about yourself?"

I turned slightly in my seat to look back at our newest student.

"Well, I was born in Saudi Arabia," he said. He seemed nervous, a little bit uncomfortable. "But my parents moved us to England when I was eleven years old. I graduated school and was in my first year at university."

"How old are you?" I asked before I could think if that was rude or not.

"Nineteen," he reported. "I first noticed something was wrong with me when I was eight years old."

He hadn't even shared the story yet, but instantly the mood in the car fell to a darker tone.

"We had a dog, my parents bought him when I was only two years old," he said. Nervously, he played with the hem of his tunic. "He was playing outside. We had a fence, but he was always escaping. I heard him yelp and ran outside. He'd been run over by a truck. He was laying in the street. He was badly injured, and he wasn't…all in one piece. It was obvious he was dead." Aleem sucked in a shaky breath. "But when I touched him, he…woke back up."

Goosebumps flashed out over every single inch of my skin.

"Even though he was broken and not in the shape he should be, my dog was once again alive," Aleem said. He sounded scared. Scared of himself. "For ten minutes, he yelped and cried, and I didn't know what to do. So, I tried to pet him to comfort him, to ease his pain. But as soon as I touched him once more, he dropped to the ground again, once more dead."

A shot of cold raced through my whole body.

"When I was sixteen, I got into a heated argument with my father," Aleem continued his tale. I could hear the quake in his voice. He was nervous to tell us all of this. I couldn't blame him. We were strangers. "I don't even remember what it was about. But he grabbed me by the shoulders. I was angry. I pushed him back, yelling and screaming. And suddenly he just…" he paused, squeezing his eyes closed. "Collapsed. I was shocked for a few moments, but finally I came to my senses. I checked for a pulse. But there wasn't one."

I shook my head in sympathy, utterly speechless.

"Everyone thought it was a heart attack," Aleem said. "I knew what had happened. But how could I explain it? I didn't understand what I had done. I thought perhaps I was a demon, a cursed being. I was afraid if I said something, they would either lock me in a mental institution, or kill me. So, I let them believe it. And I always wore gloves after that. I never touched my mother again. I tried at all costs to never come into skin to skin contact with another person. I know my touch does not always kill, but how could I ever risk it?"

My eyes fell to the black gloves he wore on his hands.

"When I graduated high school, my mother decided to move back to Saudi Arabia to be with my grandmother and her sisters. I chose to stay in England, because I thought it was safer for her that way. I'd just finished my first year at university when I ran into Borden and his glowing pencil."

I gave a little smile, but it was an automatic response.

"I thought I was the only one of my kind. That I was cursed. That I was just a freak. But then Borden explained that there were others like me, who had abilities like I do."

I nodded. "You're not alone, Aleem. Our kind was nearly hunted into extinction, but we're coming back. We're stronger and smarter. And you're not alone."

"We've never met a necromancer before you," Borden clarified. "But we have heard of them, though it wasn't from a source that we could confirm in any way. But now we know for sure. We met a man in Germany who claimed his ancestors were necromancers, and that a necromancer cannot be trained, they are born with that specific ability. So, even among our kind, you are unique, Aleem."

From the look on his face, I didn't think that was comforting to him.

Some people just want to fit in. Standing out is painful.

I just hoped we could help him to see that what made him different was what made him wonderful.

Nathaniel turned the corner and we pulled up to the gate of the Nightingale Academy. He rolled down the window and punched in the code. The gate beeped and swung open, and he slowly pulled down the driveway.

"This is where you live?" Aleem asked in wonder.

"This is the Nightingale Academy," I said with a proud smile, taking it all in. It really was spectacular now. The grounds were fully blooming, encouraged by Marie and Peter's efforts. "This is your home too, now."

Nathaniel parked in the garage and we all climbed out. We retrieved our luggage and stepped into the house.

I had to wonder about Aleem's background, considering his awe as he looked at the house. Sometimes you just never knew what was in a person's past.

"Come on," I said, tipping my head after the others. "We'll show you to your room."

"Are you sure?" he questioned. "How…how can you just take me in like this? You do not even know me."

I paused and looked back at him. It had bit us before, trusting a stranger. We'd taken Olin in without a second question. We had been so desperate.

But I didn't want to live with questions always in my mind.

"It's a feeling," I said, being honest. "I have to trust my gut. And it's telling me that you're exactly what we're looking for in this family. So, we'll take you in, and if you trust us, we'll trust you."

In his eyes, I could see just how much my words meant to him. And I knew. He hadn't trusted himself in a very long time. So a stranger, someone he could possibly kill if he accidentally touched, trusting him, meant everything.

"Thank you," he said simply in a small breath.

I just nodded, offering him a small smile, and waved for him to follow me up the stairs to his new bedroom.

CHAPTER SEVEN

A PACKAGE ARRIVED AT THE HOUSE THE VERY NEXT morning. There was a loud knock on the door and when I opened it, the person delivering it was walking down the drive. On the porch, a big brown pouch was waiting.

Just as I was about to pick it up, a smaller hand snatched it away.

I straightened to find Mary-Beth grinning down at it. She turned on the spot and walked back into the house.

"What's that?" I asked as I followed after her.

She walked to the dining table and ripped into the packaging. She pulled out a thick stack of pages. They were clipped into eight different bundles.

"Genealogical charts," Mary-Beth responded, looking through the papers with excitement. "I sent out for them two weeks ago and Grandma's genealogists just got them back to me."

"That quick?" I asked, looking down at them in amazement. The top one had an official-looking title, declaring it to be the report on John Hunsaker, as well as the extent of all living relatives they'd found.

"They didn't even bat an eye at the request," Mary-Beth said as she thumbed through John's report. "Grandma has always thought blood mattered. I just told them the names and their birthdays, and boom! Full report."

She was right. There was John at the bottom of the page, and then there were his parents, his grandparents, and dozens of others, going back. There were eight pages of ancestors, and the names and dates went clear back to 1421. The next page had a list of all his known relatives who were still alive.

"Who knows which of his ancestors was the mage," Mary-Beth said. "There are a lot of possibilities in here. But that's part of the fun, right? Figuring it out. It's like a real-life mystery puzzle."

I smiled, feeling my chest warm as I met her eyes for a moment. But she excitedly turned to the page with his relatives who were alive.

"And now we have, what? Twenty names to go investigate, see if they have mage blood, too. This is how we expand," she said.

I shook my head and pulled her into a hug. "This is really amazing, Mary-Beth."

She huffed out a laugh as I let her go. We both

looked down at the other packets in the stack. There was one for Julie and Marie. One for Dorian. Poppy. Peter, Alexandra, Abigale, and Thomas.

"I figure I can't do magic," Mary-Beth said, her tone getting more serious. "And maybe I never will be able to do it. We have a lot of ground to cover, so I think we have to be flexible with our expectations on that one. But I'm good at *this*. I like finding where we came from and who our distant cousins are. I like tracking down those who might be one of us. I want to see the school expand."

Goosebumps flashed over my arms, and something tingled in my scalp.

We had found it. Mary-Beth's place here.

We'd found our admissions officer and recruitment officer, all in one.

"This is what I want to do, Margot," she said, and for the first time, there was hope and pride in her eyes.

"And I think you're going to be the reason we flourish and aren't alone," I said. Emotions welled in my eyes, because I was so relieved. I wanted Mary-Beth to feel just how needed she was, and so far, she hadn't seen herself that way. "I think you're going to be amazing."

It was all there in her eyes. How proud she finally was of herself. She'd found her place in the grand scheme of things. And so she gave me a smile, and pulled me into a hug once more.

And just one more thing clicked into place.

. . .

CLASSES WENT EXCEPTIONALLY WELL that day. They were beautifully balanced between the first and second semester students. They were all catching on exceptionally well. Aleem immediately made friends with Peter, and already I could see his self-confidence growing.

So, by the time Nathaniel, Borden, Mary-Beth and myself gathered in my office, I was feeling confident.

We poured through our notes. We discussed our ideas. We wrote new notes down.

And in the end, we all agreed that we needed something of Olin's to help us track him.

So, at eleven o'clock that night, the four of us set off down the road toward the housing on Alderidge's property.

Olin had secured lodging at one of the student housing buildings in exchange for work there. He cleaned and took out the trash and fixed things when reckless college students broke them. It had only been three weeks since Olin had tried to kill me after I finally remembered what he'd done. We had to hope that they hadn't tossed his things out yet.

Together, we made our way across the empty lawn. Borden held a single book in his gloved hand, a small black one that we'd found in Germany.

With every step we took, taking us closer and closer to the building, memories started rising to the surface.

Over the course of two days, I had read the journal of one Katherine Dowdle. She spoke of her own views and how she did not want to live in the shadows. And one day, she met a man who believed the same as she did. They'd fought to bring the mages into the light, but in the end, it sparked a witch hunt that got almost her entire family killed.

That man, Bealdor Rayburn, was Olin.

I'd gotten chills when I realized how Olin's story aligned with Euan Sandris, a powerful mage who believed that magic shouldn't exist. He'd hunted our kind and stole their magic. And one day, he performed a rite that locked half of all magic users.

Despite being one of the most powerful mages of his day, Olin Rayburn had avoided Euan Sandris. Until his wife lost her ability to use her magic. Until she felt worthless and took her own life.

Olin had hunted him after that. And perhaps I should have been grateful for that. Sandris was wrong and had done a terrible thing. Had Nathaniel fallen into such a deep depression over losing his magic that he had taken his own life, I surely would have hunted Sandris down as well.

They had dueled it out, and in the end, Sandris sealed Olin in a book for over two and a half centuries. But the act had burned up the last bit of not just his magic, but Sandris' very life.

I'd learned all of that truth, realized how many witch

hunts Olin had spurred. I saw all the same warning signs leading me and my family toward danger.

Olin wanted to bring us out into the light. He wanted to expose the mages and to show the world just how powerful we were.

And when I had confronted him, he'd attacked.

Olin had control over metal. He'd pulled nails and doorknobs and all sorts of things from the buildings around us and sent them to kill me. I'd protected myself with my own affinity—earth. But it had been a fierce fight around campus that took us down to the beach and ended with Nathaniel unknowingly catching us and me passing out. Olin had stolen my memories, and I'd lain unconscious for six entire months.

It all washed through me as I looked at that building where he had so innocently lived.

"Anyone have any idea where he was living in the building?" I asked as we walked toward it.

"Most of these buildings are the same," Mary-Beth said. "Kitchen, living room, maintenance area, all on the first floor. The student rooms are up above. Our housekeeper had a room on the first floor. I'd guess this one isn't much different."

Only a few weeks ago, Mary-Beth was living in the building right next to this. And now she'd permanently moved into the Academy.

I could hardly imagine it any other way.

We reached the door and, finding it locked, Nathaniel worked on manipulating it until it opened.

Borden removed his glove, and the second his skin touched the book, he was entirely invisible.

"Don't forget," I said in a whisper. "It will make you invisible, but anyone can still hear you."

They all nodded and we each reached out to touch the book as well. One by one, we each disappeared from view.

We stepped inside and closed the door behind us. Together, we shuffled through the entryway, out into the open living room.

This was a boys' living unit. And it was obvious in all the décor. Leather and deep reds and strong blues. There was a dart board on the far wall with a hundred holes in the wall surrounding it. The carpet was well worn and there were stains splattered all throughout the room. It smelled strongly of alcohol. We moved beyond that into the dining room. There was a huge table with all mismatched chairs. There was a kitchen with a sink full of dishes and a smattering of messes across the countertops.

It gave me hope that they hadn't hired anyone new. If the house was this much of a mess, and that had been Olin's job, maybe they hadn't even really noticed that he had been missing for a few weeks.

We found a mechanical room and several closets. We'd all frozen in place when we heard footsteps upstairs, but it was followed by the sound of a toilet flushing just moments later.

We continued on and found a bathroom.

And then the very next room we opened revealed a bedroom with a bed that was made and things left out, abandoned.

"Bingo," Mary-Beth whispered.

We stepped inside and Nathaniel closed the door behind us. Out of view, we each let go of the book and set to searching around.

Olin truly had just disappeared. All of his clothes were still hanging in the wardrobe. His brush was sitting on the desk, as well as a notebook with a pen. There were about fifteen pages that had been ripped out of it.

"You think he came back for whatever was written in here?" Nathaniel asked.

I nodded, trying to keep quiet.

There was a spare pair of shoes under the bed, but nothing else. There weren't any books. Nothing personal in the space. Olin was tidy and didn't own much of anything considering he didn't have any kind of a job outside of keeping up this house.

I felt disappointed. It would have been nice to catch a break and find…anything useful here. But there was nothing outside of what we would find in any other bedroom.

"This is thoroughly disappointing," Borden noted.

"The man had no money and it had only been a

year," Nathaniel said, always the voice of calm and reason. "I'm almost surprised he had this many things."

"We gave him most of this shit," Borden pointed out.

It was true. Half of the clothes in the closet had been given to Olin by Borden, Nathaniel, or my father.

"Doesn't matter," I said, getting us back on track. "We need something of his. Something with DNA I would guess. Let's just get some things and get out of here before we get caught for being as loud as a herd of elephants."

Everyone shut up and we each grabbed something. We stuffed them into the bag Nathaniel had brought and then we each touched the book once more before Mary-Beth pushed open the door.

There was a young man standing at the end of the hall, just at the bottom of the steps. He peered through the dark, right at us, his eyes squinted.

Every one of us froze and no one breathed.

The young man started walking down the hall, quiet and soft.

I wanted to swear. My heart started hammering fast and hard.

Mary-Beth tugged us forward and pulled us all right down the hall, just as the man reached Olin's door. He brushed right passed Nathaniel's shoulder before stepping in the room.

I glanced over my shoulder as we quietly shuffled

down the hall. The man stepped into Olin's room and looked around.

By the time we reached the front door, we were out of view, so we dared to open it and step outside. Quietly, we closed it behind us and made sure we were a dozen steps away from the building before anyone dared to speak.

"That was amazing!" Mary-Beth declared, barely keeping her voice down. "He was looking straight at us!"

And for just a little while, we were all a couple of younger twenty something year olds, feeling like we'd gotten away with sneaking into a cookie jar.

And now we had what we needed.

We just had to find a way to make the spell work.

CHAPTER EIGHT

I hated that I was distracted and that I almost didn't want to go do this.

The very next morning, Mom showed up at eight o'clock, perky and excited.

I'd still been in bed, utterly exhausted from working half the night with the others on the tracking spell.

We hadn't gotten it yet, but we'd made good progress.

"What are you still doing in bed?" Mom asked as she walked right into our bedroom.

Blearily, I opened an eye at her, confused and disoriented. Nathaniel rolled over and held a hand up, blocking the light.

"Mom," I said, groggily. "What are you doing here? No classes today."

"I return after being missing for five years and my

daughter immediately forgets that we'd agreed to go wedding dress shopping?"

I groaned, rolled onto my back and scrubbed my hands over my face. "I'm sorry, Mom. I totally forgot. We were up late working on a tracking spell."

"And you just decided to leave me out of that?" she asked with mock indignation.

I chuckled and rolled out of bed, headed for the closet. "Technically you are a first semester student," I pointed out. "And we don't typically involve them with dangerous psychopaths who want to expose our kind."

She made a disapproving sound. "We'll talk about this later. You hurry up and get ready, so we don't miss our appointment."

I smirked at her and watched her walk out of the room. She started calling for Mary-Beth and Poppy the second she was out.

"This is…" Nathaniel trailed off. He'd propped himself up on his elbow and watched me picking clothes. "Different, having your mother around. I never thought I'd be learning to balance life with a mother-in-law. It's kind of wonderful."

I smirked at him and walked to the side of the bed. I leaned over and pressed a kiss to his lips, lingering long. "Just wait until she starts lecturing you about the propriety of us sleeping in the same bed without being married. And she'll probably do it in German or Italian, or maybe even Hungarian."

"At least if it's in German I can keep up," he said, smiling against my lips.

I smiled too, and then walked into the bathroom to get ready for the day.

Twenty minutes later, the four of us women walked out into the garage, climbed into my new vehicle, and headed toward the dress shop.

"I have to admit," Mary-Beth said as we walked up to the doors. "There are few people on this planet who look good in a suit every day, but that is Nathaniel to a tee. I can hardly even imagine what he's going to look like in a tux."

Playfully, I punched her in the arm. "That's my fiancé you're talking about. Get your own."

"Hey," she said playfully, holding up her hands in surrender. "I'm just complimenting. Well done, Margot. And I'm working on the man thing. I may or may not have an interest in Thomas."

My mouth opened in a gape. "You will be spilling your guts when this is over."

She smirked. "Of course. But for now…I would never steal your thunder."

"Ladies, ladies," Mom chided as we stepped inside the shop. There were very few people around and there was soft music playing. "Let's focus now."

Right then, a woman with a measuring tape draped around her neck walked up and introduced herself. Her name went in one ear and out the other immediately.

"How about you take a look around at what we have and you can pick out a few styles you like, and then you can start trying on some dresses?" she asked with a well-practiced smile. "And congratulations on the engagement."

"Thank you," I offered with a smile.

And it really started to hit me then.

Nathaniel and I were actually engaged. I had his ring on my finger. We'd broken through all the awkwardness of our relationship and the fights and insecurities, and here we were.

We'd committed to spending the rest of our lives together.

We would have babies together someday and raise those children. Someday those kids would go to high school, and they'd get in trouble and Nathaniel and I would have to get creative in guiding them.

This was real life. Just like my parents got married twenty-five years ago, Nathaniel and I were doing this.

A smile pulled on my lips. It was scary when I really thought about it.

But I was so ready.

We weren't sweet and quiet and calm as we went through the dress store. We laughed and talked and dramatically held ridiculous dresses up to our frames. It was so much fun, and we were all having the best time.

Finally, I had five dresses I liked and headed into the dressing room.

I laughed to myself as I tried on the first. It literally made me look like I was pregnant.

I walked out, and both Mom and Mary-Beth started laughing immediately. Poppy just smiled, her lips pressed together, too polite to laugh at me.

I went back in and tried on the second dress.

This one was short, and only came to my knees. It was silk and had a sweetheart neckline.

I walked out.

Mary-Beth made a face. "It's cute, but this is your wedding, not a prom."

"Exactly," Mom said, nodding in agreement.

"I have to agree with them," Poppy pitched in.

Once more I returned to the dressing room.

With the next one on, I stepped out.

It reached the floor and was mermaid shaped, fanning out around my feet.

I felt disappointed the moment I tried it on. I'd really thought this would be the one.

Poppy's look of disappointment echoed my own.

"I hate to say it, honey, but you're much too short for that dress," Mom said.

"Yep," Mary-Beth agreed. "Pretty sure you'd need to be at least five-foot eight to make that dress work."

"You mean her five-foot three frame can't pull it off?" Poppy joked.

"Hey, I'm the bride here," I scolded them, trying not to laugh. "You're supposed to be nice to me."

"Oh, you look beautiful, honey," Mom said quickly, nodding her head.

I just rolled my eyes at her and turned to walk back into the dressing room.

I peeled the dress off and took the next off the hanger. And as I pulled it on, I felt goosebumps flash over my entire body.

I looked at myself in the mirror, and something zinged from my scalp down to my toes.

With a deep breath, I turned, and walked out.

"Oh, Margot," Mom breathed.

"Yes," Mary-Beth said with a grin and a nod.

"That is the magic," Poppy let out with wide eyes.

The skirt of the dress was full. Really full. It was lace and the back was stacked with layers of it. It gathered tight around my waist, and the bodice hugged me tightly up and over my bust. Tank straps rose up and over my shoulders, and then it laced up in the back.

"Margot, that dress is stunning," Mom said as she stood up and came to stand in front of me.

I turned, looking at myself in the mirrors behind me.

I looked…like a princess. Yet I also felt sexy, and surprisingly…extremely confident.

Looking at myself in the mirror, I felt like a bride.

"Nathaniel is going to lose his mind," Poppy said as she walked up beside me, looking at my reflection in the mirror.

"For all of five minutes before he rips it off your body," Mary-Beth added before setting a veil in my hair.

"I like you most days, Mary-Beth Foster," Mom said with the shake of her head. "And then you go and say things like that."

We all laughed, but I was having a hard time not blushing, because I was absolutely imagining it. Nathaniel in a tux, me in this dress. Being alone after the wedding. I pictured him undoing the laces in the back. The way it would fall to the floor.

And all the things that would follow after.

"Margot!" Mom chided.

Looking at myself in the mirror, I was blushing, hard, but also, it was very obvious in my eyes what I was thinking about.

"What?" I defended myself. "We've been head over heels for each other for nearly two years now and we've never done the deed. I'm a little anxious for this next part, okay?"

It was ridiculous and we were loud and a little crazy. But it was truly one of the best days of my life.

And in the end, I walked out of the shop with the dress I would say *I do* in, carefully tucked away in a huge dress bag, slung over my arm.

CHAPTER NINE

WE ALL STARED AT THE GLOBE, WATCHING AS LITTLE lights flashed on the surface of it.

Here in Harrington. A few places in England. Somewhere in Germany. A quick blip in China.

"It's not working," Borden said.

Nathaniel folded his arms over his chest and stared at the blinking magical lights. "I think it's working to some degree. Just…not in the way we want it to."

We were all gathered up in my office. The daylight outside was fading, the sky falling from blue to pink to orange. We'd spent the last four nights solid working on the tracking spell, and tonight, we'd finally put it into action.

The lights were supposed to show us Olin's location on the globe.

"Perhaps it's all the locations he's ever been," I

suggested. "He's been here in Harrington," I said, pointing at the blinking light on our location. "We know he is from England and has been there recently." I pointed at England on the globe as well. "And we know he can use portal magic. So, he easily could have gone to Germany and China."

"This is why she's in charge," Mary-Beth said in a nod. "All hail Queen Margot."

I cast a look at her and shook my head but fought a small smile. Mary-Beth gave a little bow.

"That seems most likely," Nathaniel said in agreement. "If only we could somehow make it give us a timeline."

Borden stared at the globe, a hand covering his mouth as he considered.

We were close. So, so close to getting this.

We needed it to work now. Just this morning, my father had come over and shown us another newspaper article. Another political leader had been found murdered, killed in the same way, the body magically levitating in the air.

Two deaths now. Olin was responsible for two deaths.

And now I felt responsible for at least one of those. If only we could find Olin, somehow, we could stop him.

The doorbell rang and everyone looked toward the door as Khan started barking down below.

"That's for us," Borden said, his eyes rising up to meet mine.

I gave him a look of confusion, but he just nodded for me to follow him, so I set off after him down the stairs.

"It's going to put us at risk if you continue going to the jewelers to sell the gold," Borden explained as we walked down the spiral staircase. "Eventually they're going to question where you're getting it from and they may alert the authorities." We hooked onto the next set of stairs and descended to the main floor.

"I've arranged for a buyer to come here," Borden said as he looked back at me. "I've run a background check on him, vetted him thoroughly. *You* can trust him."

The way he emphasized that *I* could trust him made me wonder if the *authorities* would trust him.

But I trusted Borden with my life, so I would trust that I could trust someone he trusted.

"He's agreed to come once a week and he will buy all the gold you have," Borden continued to explain as we crossed to the front door. "He will be paying in cash. And he will keep coming every week until you tell him to stop."

It was a lot to process. I would have loved to have a few moments to process it all and ask questions. But there was no time as Borden grabbed the handle of the front door and pulled it open. I grabbed Khan by the collar to hold him back.

There was a man standing on the porch. He looked to be in his mid-forties. He wore a tidy black suit and sported a well-cared for salt and pepper beard. And in his left hand, he carried an oversized, black briefcase.

"Come in," Borden invited the man. He stepped inside and Borden closed the door behind him. "Mr. Wellington, this is Margot. Margot, this is Mr. Wellington."

"Pleasure to meet you," the man said simply.

"You too," I said, and it sounded just a little bit ingenuine considering that Borden had taken me totally off guard.

I waited for there to be more talk. For there to be explanations or some kind of agreement made. But they both just looked at me. So, I nodded my head awkwardly. "I'll be right back."

I walked back into my bedroom, taking the puppy with me. I deposited him in my bedroom, and as I closed the door behind me, I realized how terrible my hiding place was. I literally got down on my hands and knees and pulled the lock box out from beneath the bed. I grabbed the keys from their hiding place in the bathroom and walked back out.

Borden and Mr. Wellington had moved to the dining table. There was a scale set up and Mr. Wellington waited patiently.

I set the lock box down on the table and opened it. And I started taking out my golden rocks one at a time.

I had continued to do alchemy every single day. One or two rocks a day, I had done the magic and watched as they'd transformed. I'd added them to the collection one at a time.

With Borden gone so much lately, I hadn't even wanted to go sell it. It just didn't feel the same.

But here he was, home once more, helping me to take care of the mages.

Mr. Wellington weighed the rocks one at a time and made a list of their weight on a pad of paper. When he was all done, he added it up. He then opened his briefcase, and I got a quick glimpse of sleeves of money before he turned it, so the lid blocked our view.

Carefully, he counted. And then he handed it over to me.

"I think you will find my prices very fair," he said.

I quickly looked through it, and he was right. He was giving me a very fair amount for the gold.

This was enough to support the academy and our needs for at least three months.

"Yes," I agreed. "Thank you."

"Thank you for your business," Mr. Wellington said as he loaded the gold into his briefcase and closed it. "I will see you again next week."

We walked him to the door and saw him out. When the door closed, I looked up at Borden.

"Thank you," I said, truly meaning it. "This...this will make everything so much easier."

"You're welcome, Margot," Borden offered.

And in his voice, I heard everything. That his feelings

had not faded. That this was still just as hard on him. But that we were still friends.

I didn't know what else to do. I loved Borden. I always would. Because when it came down to it, he was loyal and true. But I didn't want to hurt him. I wanted him to be happy. I just didn't know what else I could do to change any of it.

I could create the gold. But because of him, we would get the money from it that would take care of us forever.

CHAPTER TEN

The next morning, the phone rang in the living room. I walked out of my bedroom and grabbed it.

"Hello?"

"I'm looking for Borden Stewart," a young woman's voice came through on the other end. "Is he there?"

"He is," I said, my brows furrowed. No one ever called for Borden. "Can I tell him who is calling?"

"Chloe Stewart," she answered, leaving me frozen and speechless for too long.

Borden's much younger sister.

"Yes, just a minute," I said. Carefully, I set the phone down on the table and darted up the stairs. I walked down the hall to the bedroom on the end. I knocked loudly on the door before letting myself inside.

This was one of those absolutely rare days when I

woke before Borden. He propped himself up on his elbow, squinting through the dim light at me.

"What's wrong?" he asked.

"It's your sister," I said, shocked myself. "She's on the phone."

His eyes widened at that and he scrambled up from the bed. I had to turn away because Borden was wearing his underwear and nothing more. Quickly, he threw a shirt on and walked out the door. He rushed past me and shuffled down the stairs so quick I worried he might trip and fall.

Slowly, I followed. I wanted to give him space and privacy. But I was also wildly curious.

Borden hadn't spoken to his family in a year and a half. Not since he left the Society Boys and started hanging out with Nathaniel and me. He'd cut ties with them and they'd disowned him.

I walked into the kitchen to start making breakfast, forcing myself not to listen to the conversation Borden was quietly having on the phone.

Eggs. Bacon. Potatoes.

We didn't need all this food. None of us were heavy breakfast eaters. But my mind went into auto pilot of doing too much to distract myself.

The potatoes were frying on the stove and I was scrambling the eggs when Nathaniel walked out of the bedroom, just at the same time as Borden said goodbye and hung up.

I couldn't help it. I turned toward him, and our eyes fixed on each other.

"Is everything okay?" I asked.

Borden's face was stone white, so I knew the answer already.

He shook his head. "My father has had a stroke," he said. "He's not doing well. They don't think he's going to make it." His voice was rough, the words barely escaping his throat. "He's asked to see me."

I didn't know what to say. Borden was independent and had always been able to take care of himself. But I could tell how much it hurt him that his father had cut him off.

And now he'd asked to see Borden.

My eyes shifted past Borden to meet Nathaniel's eyes, and in them, I could see that he also understood how monumental this was.

"I…" Borden hesitated. "I need to catch a plane."

"Who knows when there will be a connecting flight," Nathaniel said. "I'll drive you."

"It's a four-hour drive to New York City," Borden said, turning slightly to look at Nathaniel.

My fiancé nodded his head. "It will still be faster than trying to get a flight."

I could see the look of appreciation in Borden's eyes. Finally, he just nodded. "Thank you."

Borden strode off to the stairs to go pack a bag and Nathaniel came to my side in the kitchen.

"That was very sweet of you to offer," I said as I stirred the potatoes.

Nathaniel shrugged. "This is a big deal. I imagine he's going to need some time to process. The drive will give him that without any distractions."

I grabbed the front of his shirt and pulled him toward me. I tipped up on my toes and pressed my lips gently to his. "You're a good person, Nathaniel Nightingale."

"You bring out the best in me," he said softly against my lips.

I tried to offer Borden a plate of food when he came back down five minutes later but knew what his answer was going to be.

"No, thank you," he said distractedly. He shifted his bag from one hand to the other nervously.

"Take as much time as you need," I said as I quickly kissed Nathaniel goodbye.

"I'll call you when I can," he promised. Then I watched them walk out the door, and they were gone.

I went for a walk with Khan that night to distract myself.

Nathaniel had called just after lunch. They'd reached the hospital where Borden's father was. Borden had gone in to see him and just a few moments come back out and told Nathaniel that he could go home. Borden would fly home when he was ready.

Nathaniel was turning around and would be back home at some point tonight.

I wandered down the sidewalk with the puppy and automatically found myself turning toward the university. As I stepped onto the grounds, everything rushed back to me. Growing up on this campus, following my parents around, visiting their classrooms. And then my semester and a half as a student here. The stress of classes and tests, but also the boredom, because I knew everything those first few classes could teach me.

It all felt like forever ago.

But it was nice to walk through the campus. There were a few students out playing a game on the grounds. It was still summer, so it was exceptionally quiet. There were a few essential courses taught in the summer semester, but it was bare bones. Most students went back home this time of year.

So, there was little activity going on as I cut down the sidewalks. The air was just the right temperature and there was a slight breeze. I wore a light dress and it was just the right level of comfort on a day like today.

I found myself walking through the arch that led to the stairs that descended to the beach. I threw a ball for Khan and he went bounding after it. I found a large rock, and sat on it, hugging my knees to my chest.

Time was going too quickly lately. I felt like we weren't getting enough done some days. We were already a third of the way through our semester. We hadn't found

Olin yet. My wedding was only two months away. I'd be twenty-one before long.

Summer would be gone in a blink and suddenly I would be all grown up.

Not that I'd ever felt much like a kid.

"I thought that was you, Margot Bell."

The voice from behind sent me jumping from my rock to stand. And as I turned and met his eyes, everything in me went prickly and cold.

"Oh, hell," I breathed. "Go away, David."

Khan barked protectively and came to stand beside me.

Like the annoyance ghost from the past, David Sinclair stood there, looking me up and down like it was the first week of my freshman year.

"What kind of greeting is that for a friend you haven't seen in a year?" he asked with a smirk as he walked up.

"We were never friends, David," I said. "You're just an entitled asshole who thinks everyone worships the ground you walk on."

"Well, when you're nearly god-like…" he trailed off. He walked up, his eyes boring into me. He reached out and grabbed a lock of my hair, observing it.

I immediately swatted his hand away, sending a little extra magical zing into it.

Khan barked loudly and took a step toward David.

He dropped his hand with a little hiss, but still held onto his smirk. "Still just as much fire," he said, undeterred. "My offer still stands. You and I together could take over the whole of the New England area."

My eyes narrowed at him. "Sorry you're still having trouble conning a woman into being with you, but it's still far too late." I held up my hand with Nathaniel's ring on it.

David barely even looked at it. His eyes shifted out over the ocean. "Mine would have been at least four karats. If you're going to put a ring on it, might as well make sure the entire world knows for damn sure you're claimed."

I rolled my eyes, my entire body filled to the brim with annoyance. "What are you even doing back here, David?"

He smiled, still looking out at the ocean. "I've taken over the roll as the Society Boy's advisor for the upcoming semester. I was just meeting with Dean Lowell about my new plans and ideas for the events this fall. Guess you'll be seeing more of me around."

My stomach dropped out and I felt sick. "I thought you lived in Chicago now?"

"That was just an internship, darling," he said, offering me a smile. "Boston became my home as of two weeks ago. The firm was looking for a hungry new partner."

I groaned. Suddenly Boston was far, far too close.

"So how long did it last?" David asked as he turned toward me, standing far too close. "Borden? I always knew he made a mistake joining your strange little crew."

A smirk finally grew on my face now. "Borden's like family. He lives with us now. My fiancé took him to visit his father today, actually."

That got me a look of surprise from David. I felt far too much satisfaction that things worked out the way they did.

"I always wondered what weird shit Borden was in to," David said. "Never pegged you as a polygamist though, Margot."

The crunch of sand behind me turned both our attention. There, we saw Nathaniel walking up with Mary-Beth, Poppy, and Thomas. Khan barked, happy to see Nathaniel, and bounded over to him.

"David," Nathaniel said, his tone filled with surprise. "You are about the last person I ever expected to see here on the beaches of Harrington."

"Margot was just catching me up on the twisted antics of your nightlife," David said. "Are these some of the other players? Is it an all-night love fest in that grungy solarium you call a home?"

I took a step forward, ready to put hands on David, but Nathaniel reached out and grabbed my wrist, stopping me.

"Having so many hot lies in your mouth might get you far in the business world, David," Nathaniel said, his tone low and even. He looked down at David from his height, being a good seven inches taller, "But when you find yourself alone in your penthouse at night, know the only one to blame is yourself."

"Perhaps you haven't bothered to take a ride through town," I said, because I was getting filled with familiar hot coals. "But the Asteria House looks a little different these days. You might have gotten me kicked out of school, but I found a way to make it all on my own, David Sinclair. You should see my house now. But I would never invite such a sad, foul-mouthed little prick into our home."

The look in David's eyes darkened and he leaned forward into Nathaniel's face. "At least now you have somewhere clean to lay your sugar mommy down."

I hardly even processed what happened, it was over so fast.

Nathaniel's arm cocked back and shot forward with a fist.

He caught David square in the face, and David tripped backward into the sand. He clutched his nose and I could see the blood oozing out between his fingers.

Everyone gave out shouts of surprise and shock and Khan nearly lost his mind.

Nathaniel didn't hesitate. He walked over and squatted down in the sand right beside David. "No one likes a bully," he said as David stared up at Nathaniel in shock. "You're a university graduate. You have a career. You should know that by now. I tolerated your antics for three years, David. I truly don't want to ever see your face again. But if I do, know that I'm done being patient. This was your warning."

Nathaniel stood and extended a hand down to David to help him up. But David just scrambled back in the sand to get away from Nathaniel. He awkwardly got to his feet, staring at Nathaniel like he was afraid he was going to hit him again. Blood continued to gush from his most likely broken nose.

"Freaks," David said meekly as he stepped onto the first steps.

"Oh, David," I called. "You're going to quit that Society Boy advisor position, right? And stay the hell out of Harrington?"

He simply glared darkly at us, then turned and swiftly walked up the stairs and out of sight. But something told me that I wouldn't have to manipulate his mind to get him to stay far, far away from here.

"That…" Mary-Beth trailed off, "was truly amazing."

"Finally," Thomas said. "After watching that guy be an ass to you for years, you finally put him in his place. I had no idea you had that in you. One punch and he was down and out?"

I just smiled and shook my head as Nathaniel turned red and his expression grew sheepish. "There are reasons I let David push me around. You have no idea how much self-control it took to only punch once."

"Well, if it was only once, it was a damn good one!"

Thomas cheered with pride as he clapped an arm over Nathaniel's shoulders. We all turned, and slowly started making our way down the beach.

"Was Nathaniel some kind of arena fighter when he was younger?" Poppy asked innocently.

I chuckled at that, even if the truth was no laughing matter. "Not exactly. But let's just say there are two very different sides to Nathaniel. The side you just saw was his past, but every now and then, it creeps out."

"It was epic!" Thomas said, still thrilled at the bloodshed.

"Violence is never the answer," Nathaniel advised. "At least that's what they say."

Thomas cheered at that.

I noticed Mary-Beth looking over at Thomas admiringly. And noted when he looked over at her and his cheeks turned pink.

Nathaniel dropped back and took my hand as we walked through the sand. In his other, he held Khan's leash. He was growing more massive by the moment.

"Thanks for saving the day," I said. "You may have potentially saved me from a murder charge."

He laughed and leaned over, pressing a kiss to the top of my head. "I have no doubt it was David I saved. Not you, Margot."

I grinned at that. Nathaniel never underestimated me, and that was one of the things I loved most about him.

"How's Borden?" I asked, watching as the others made their way up the beach, back toward home.

"Somber," Nathaniel said. "I went up to the room with him, but didn't go inside, so I can't speak for how his father is. But Borden was very quiet on the ride up. I could tell he was conflicted about the encounter."

I shook my head. "I don't know what this encounter is going to lead to. But I'm glad he gets to see his family. It's so tragic that it all just imploded the way it did."

Nathaniel nodded in agreement.

And a thought hit me. "Have you ever considered it? Going and looking for your biological family? At least your brother and sister?"

Nathaniel paused for the briefest moment, but it was enough to tell me everything. "No," he answered honestly. "I…I haven't even thought about it."

But they were out there. Who knew what they were like? They could be anyone. Could live any kind of life.

It was bizarre to think that he wouldn't even recognize them if he saw them on the street. He was only three years old the last time he saw them.

I looked up at Nathaniel, and now I could see the wheels turning in his head.

Because reunification with his family wasn't the only possible outcome.

They shared his blood. And there was magic in Nathaniel's blood.

There would be magic in their blood, as well.

CHAPTER ELEVEN

WE DIDN'T HEAR FROM BORDEN THE NEXT DAY. Poppy was due back to work, so, not knowing what to do, she left for the airport without him. She would be gone for four days.

Nathaniel and I taught classes. Mom arrived to join the first semester students. It was actually nice, having a larger group. There were six of them, and they helped each other greatly. They could practice on each other. And they were making quick progress.

That night, Nathaniel and I debated if we wanted to involve the second semester students in helping with the tracking spell.

"I don't want to involve them with Olin," I said honestly that night as we lay in bed. "I know they saw what he can do at your graduation party. But…" I shook my head. "I would feel so responsible if any of them got hurt going up against him."

"I think it's safe to say that every one of them would die to help take him down," Nathaniel said. He propped himself up on an elbow and looked down at me. "Family always takes a little leap of trust."

"I know," I said with a sigh. "I just…it's still hard to share the burden of this. It was just you and then just you and me. We keep growing, but I still feel like it's just the two of us and we can't trust anyone else or we're going to die in a modern witch hunt."

Nathaniel leaned down, tipping my chin up to him. "I will always keep you safe, Margot," he promised. "No matter what it takes."

I reached a hand up, cupping his face as I pulled his lips down to mine. His were tender and strong at the same time, reflecting his promise. They told me how much he meant his promise.

Nathaniel reached into my soul and wrapped his strong, scarred hands around my heart. He reached into my stomach and wound his way all the way down to my toes. Our souls intertwined as I breathed him in, opening our kiss deeper and deeper.

His hand slid down my neck, over my arm, and down to my hip. He shifted his weight forward, laying himself half on top of me, and my entire body lit to life at the contact.

We'd slept in the same bed for weeks now and I'd not

grown tired of his heat lying beside me. I couldn't ever get enough of his skin and the intense look in his eyes when he stared at me across the pillow.

This was how it would be, forever. He and I, two that were always meant to be together.

I pulled Nathaniel's shirt up and over his head and ran my hands up his bare chest. He was refined muscle and toned. There were scars lining his torso and back and I knew there were stories behind them that I didn't want to exist.

But they made me appreciate his body even more. It had survived so much, but he'd still turned out this tender.

My eyes rose to meet his, dark green staring down into my blue. "I love you," I said softly in the dark.

"And I love you," Nathaniel swore as he lowered his mouth down to mine and claimed it as his for the rest of forever.

THURSDAY EVENING, we got a phone call from Borden.

His father had passed away on Wednesday. There would be a funeral on Friday. He would be returning home Sunday night. He asked for Nathaniel to pick him up from the airport.

Of course, it brought the mood down. Everyone was filled with empathy and all we wanted to do was give Borden a hug.

But Nathaniel was exceptionally quiet throughout the rest of the night. I could tell his mind was far away, lost in deep thoughts. And they were the kind that needed to be left alone, so I let him have his space.

During our lunch break on Friday, he spent the entire time on the phone. I was busy making wedding plans with Mom. We were going over the guest list. She wanted to invite half the staff of Alderidge, and I kept having to remind her that Dean Lowell was *not* invited. I wanted to keep this small and intimate. Somewhere, there was a compromise, and eventually we would get there.

Mom reminded me that we needed to get our picture taken so that an announcement could be put in the paper. We scheduled that for the next day.

That evening, after classes and after dinner was cleaned up, Nathaniel and I made our way out onto the deck. The sun was setting, casting the sky in a bright orange hue. There was a strong breeze, so there were waves crashing onto the beach below.

Nathaniel settled into one chair, and I sat in the one next to him.

He reached out and took my hand. And then he just sat there, staring out at the ocean for a long stretch of time.

I didn't know if I should be worried. Nathaniel was a thoughtful person. His head was full of history and five different languages. He was always thinking about the future of the academy and our future together.

But this felt different.

I didn't know how long it had been when he finally spoke without looking over at me.

"I made some calls today," he said. "It wasn't easy, because it's been twenty years. But they finally dug up the information for me. I got my parents' names."

Oh.

Oh.

That's what this was about.

And instantly I knew what triggered it. The death of Borden's father.

"Philip and Regina Nightingale," Nathaniel said, his chin lifting a little. "Those are the names of the people who brought me into this world."

"Nathaniel, that's…" But I didn't know what it actually was.

"Regina died eleven years ago," Nathaniel continued on, and it was almost as if he wanted the words out of him as quickly as possible. "Drug overdose. She was brought into the hospital as a Jane Doe until her sister came in and claimed her. Her ashes were given to my aunt."

That was so much to process, just in those few sentences.

"And Philip is in jail," Nathaniel continued. "Lifelong sentence for assault, possession, and attempted murder." My stomach dropped, and the words sounded as if they stuck in Nathaniel's throat. He paused, thinking things over. "Philip is such a proper name. You'd never expect a Philip to abuse and neglect his kids. To screw up so badly he lands in jail for the rest of his life."

My stomach turned. It wasn't fair. The hand Nathaniel had been dealt. Why hadn't he been born into a family who loved him enough to straighten out their lives?

With his free hand, Nathaniel reached into his pocket and pulled out a piece of paper. He held it up so he could read it.

"My brother's name is Kenneth," Nathaniel said. "And my sister is Laurel."

He let those names sink in for a moment, and they all hit me. These were siblings. There were three Nightingale siblings, and until today, Nathaniel didn't even know their names.

"The agency didn't know where they are," Nathaniel said. "They aged out of the foster system, just like me. They don't keep track of kids after that."

"But you have their names now," I said, excitement building in me. "Mary-Beth is good at this kind of thing. And if she can't find them, she knows people who can."

Finally, Nathaniel's eyes rose to meet mine. He held them for a moment, mulling over his words. "I'm scared, Margot. What if…what if they aren't good people either? What if they're dead, too? What if…what if they don't remember me?"

And in that last fear, I heard the truth. Nathaniel didn't remember them either, simply that they existed.

I shook my head. "Maybe all of those things will happen. But Nathaniel, haven't you spent the last twenty years wondering?"

He looked so scared but unsure.

"At least then you would know," I said in a breath.

He held my eyes for another long moment. And then he sat back in his seat and looked out over the ocean.

I didn't know what he had decided, or if he had even made a decision. But whatever it turned out to be, I would support him.

CHAPTER TWELVE

Nathaniel's decision was apparent Saturday morning. He and Mary-Beth were already on the phone when I woke up. They had a notepad in front of them, notes written all over it. Nathaniel looked up at me when I walked out of the bedroom and offered me this little smile that said it all.

He was going to find his brother and sister.

I left them to it.

I took a walk down to my parents' house and had breakfast with them. Mom and I went over wedding plans, figuring out the decorations. Dad tried to offer money to help pay for everything, and I kindly turned it down, reminding him that money wouldn't be a problem, ever, so long as I had access to rocks and blood, and gold didn't lose its value.

Just after lunch, I made my way back home. It looked as if Mary-Beth and Nathaniel hadn't even moved.

"He kind of doesn't seem like the person who has a family," Abigale said as she made a sandwich in the kitchen. When I looked at her sharply, her eyes widened, and she rushed to explain. "I just mean…Nathaniel seems like he's this self-contained person. Like…he just magically came into being, fully grown and formed the way he is. He's just this…professor and wise leader. You two are obviously a package, but it's hard to imagine that he has ties to anyone or anything else. That he had a past as a kid. Does that make sense?"

As I looked over at Nathaniel, talking on the phone, I gave a small shrug. "I suppose so."

But I had a realization then. Nathaniel and I had never had any wise leader we could look to and rely on.

But for everyone in this house, Nathaniel was that person.

I felt a little older then.

And I could see the legacy of what we were building. We were still so young. We had the vast majority of our lives ahead of us right now. We could continue teaching and running the academy for…sixty years. How many semesters could we teach in that time? How many generations of mages might we mentor?

And I realized then, that to some degree, this was always going to be a literal family affair. Someday Nathaniel and I would teach our children magic. But we would also teach Borden's, or Mary-Beth's, or Aleem's, or Dorian's.

And as we discovered more and more mages thanks to Mary-Beth's efforts, how large would the school get? How many mages might we re-introduce into the world?

I saw the vision of it. Of a whole population of us. Of security and safety. Maybe someday we could even establish our own community, where we would never have to hide what we are.

It was a long, long way off. But it wasn't entirely impossible.

The doorbell rang at two o'clock. When I answered it and found a photographer standing there, my eyes widened for just a moment.

I had completely forgotten that we were supposed to be getting our picture taken for the wedding announcement.

Quickly, I grabbed Nathaniel and we posed in the library. Thankfully we were at least both dressed and presentable looking. The photographer clicked away, taking at least ten shots before bidding us goodbye.

Nathaniel returned to his work with Mary-Beth. I left everyone to their tasks and wandered down to the beach. I collected five rocks and headed up to my office.

I had a wedding to pay for and a house full of mouths to feed.

I turned every one of those five rocks into gold using my blood and magic.

It was four-thirty when Nathaniel walked up into the office. I tried to read his face as he walked in and leaned against the wall. There was hope in his eyes, but also conflict.

"We found them," he said.

For several long moments, we stared at each other, letting those three words hang in the air. Because no matter what came next, it was going to change things for Nathaniel.

"Kenneth, my brother, is in jail," Nathaniel finally said, and immediately, I wished they weren't real. "Armed robbery," he continued. "He's been in for two years, has six left. Kenneth is the oldest of us. He's thirty."

Which meant he was seven years older than Nathaniel. He would have been ten when he was taken away from Regina and Philip. How much had he already seen his parents do? How much might they have involved him in their illegal activities?

Perhaps it was too late by the time the state stepped in.

"I'm so sorry, Nathaniel," I said, shaking my head.

He gave an acknowledging nod, his eyes a little bit unfocused where they stared at the floor. "It's okay. Better to know early. Means I don't have to wonder anymore."

I took a step forward and grabbed Nathaniel's hands in mine.

His eyes rose to meet mine. "We found my sister, too."

My heart leapt into my throat. How much worse could it get? He was searching for four people, and so far half of them were in jail and one was dead.

"Laurel lives in Scituate," Nathaniel said.

My mouth dropped open a little. "That's…Nathaniel, that's only thirty minutes away."

He pulled a piece of paper out of his pocket and held it up. On it, there was an address written. "I know."

I looked up into his green eyes and tried my very hardest to read them. He was so scared. But also so hopeful.

"I thought maybe I'd just drive by," he said softly. "Maybe I can catch a glimpse of what she's like. We didn't get much information, just where she lives, and that her last name is now Douglas, so I know she's either married, or has been married. I…I just want to see what she's like."

I nodded, my heart beating a hundred miles a minute. "I think that sounds like a great idea."

"Would you come with me, Margot?" he asked, his voice very soft and quiet.

"Of course," I said as I reached a hand up and caressed the side of his face. His hands gripped my hips and in them I could feel his fear as he pulled me in and kissed me.

This meant so much to him. And I tried not to imagine everything he had lost over the years, but I couldn't help it.

His entire family, and with it, so much of his identity.

He didn't even know their names. He knew nothing about his grandparents, or where his family came from, except by his own determined research into the name Nightingale.

Here was his chance.

"Let's go," he said quietly.

We asked Alexandra and Peter to keep an eye on Khan, who was now entering the chewing phase of puppyhood. We told the others that we didn't know when we would be back, to which they simply said goodbye.

I sat in the driver's seat and started the ignition. Nathaniel's mind was eighteen miles away. There was no way he could focus on the drive.

We backed down the drive and out the gate, and pulled out onto the road, headed south-east along the coast.

The miles both flew by and dragged. I was familiar enough with the area that it wasn't difficult to navigate. Scituate was only two towns away. My father frequently spoke as a guest at their community college. I'd gone with him a number of times.

The address was just two blocks from the ocean, and as we slowed to find the exact house number, Nathaniel's hands gripped his slacks harder and harder.

I parked across the street, and we both looked at the house.

It was white, like most of the houses around it. It was

two stories, and well taken care of. There was a white fence around the entire thing, and out in the small yard, I could see toys scattered around.

"Looks like she has a family," I said.

Nathaniel nodded, and just then, the side door of the house opened, and two little blonde children came spilling out, and grabbed some of the toys.

Then, a tall blonde woman walked out behind them.

Nathaniel immediately slid down in his seat, trying to get out of view, but didn't tear his eyes away from her.

"She looks just like you," I observed as she followed the little boy around the yard. And it was true. She was tall and lean like Nathaniel. Her hair was the same dirty blonde shade as his, and slightly curly as well. Her eyebrows were arched the same. She had the same mouth as him. Even the way she walked was similar to the way Nathaniel did.

I had never had any siblings. Mom and Dad talked about having more children, but it just didn't happen, whether that was because they physically couldn't or they just never fit it in, I hadn't ever asked. I couldn't even imagine what Nathaniel was feeling.

But I felt…excited. Because in just a few months, this woman would be my sister-in-law.

We watched them for a few minutes. Laurel seemed like a good mom. She laughed with the kids. She chased them around the yard. She called out to the little boy when he tried to eat a mouthful of sand. She took note of the flowers the little girl picked.

She didn't look like a drug addict. She didn't look like a criminal.

She just looked…like a mom.

"I'm scared to death to go out there," Nathaniel said. "I…as much as I really want to meet her kids…stars, they are my niece and nephew…I kind of wish it was just her this first time, you know?"

I nodded. "I get it."

"But what if I chicken out later?" he said, and I could tell he was seriously contemplating it. "I might talk myself out of it, Margot."

I didn't think so. Nathaniel was brave in quiet ways he didn't always give himself credit for.

But I didn't get the chance to tell him so, because he proved me right when he opened the car door and climbed out.

I got out as well, and just stood beside the car, watching to see what he was going to do.

Nathaniel slid his hands into his front pockets and watched them for a few more moments. As if he were doing this one, small step at a time. He leaned up against the car, and simply watched.

We caught the woman's attention. She glanced at us, and looked back at her children. And then she seemed to realize we were staring right at her. She looked our way and held still, concern growing on her brow.

When we didn't look away, when Nathaniel stood there frozen, she stood a little straighter. Nathaniel stood up, his shoulders alert and attentive. And I could just imagine how his heart started racing as she walked toward us.

"Can I help..." But as she put her hand on the gate and opened it, she trailed off. Her eyes fixed on Nathaniel. And she slowly took another step forward. She took another cautious step into the street, never looking away from Nathaniel.

She stopped right in the middle of the road, and I watched as her eyes reddened and welled.

"Nathaniel?" she asked, quiet and unsure.

Nathaniel took a step forward and nodded.

Tears broke free from Laurel's eyes. She stepped forward, taking long, bounding steps. And she didn't even hesitate as she collided with Nathaniel. She threw her arms around him and crushed him into her.

It was a testament to Nathaniel's height. Laurel was tall, but he still towered above her.

"They told me they lost track of you years ago," Laurel said, squeezing Nathaniel so tight I thought she might break him in half. "I made so many phone calls, but no one could tell me where you went."

She took half a step back and looked up into Nathaniel's eyes. I realized then that hers were the same shade of green.

They could very nearly be twins.

"I…" Nathaniel said, at a complete loss for words. "Laurel. You…" He shook his head, and I watched as emotions filled Nathaniel's own eyes.

Laurel smiled, and it stunned me. It was so bright and joyful, and it looked so much like Nathaniel's. "This is amazing," she said, confirming everything Nathaniel was feeling. "It's been, so, so long. I never thought I would see you again."

I recognized it as Nathaniel once more pulled his sister into his chest in a hug. That was relief. He had been so scared that his siblings wouldn't even recognize him, because he couldn't remember their faces, or even their names.

But Laurel had recognized him immediately. Even though he had only been three years old the last time she had seen him.

"How did you even find me?" Laurel asked, looking at her tall, little brother.

"A friend helped me," he said, finally able to form sentences. "We made a lot of phone calls."

Laurel's eyes shifted over to me, even though I wasn't the friend Nathaniel spoke of. Nathaniel took a step back and extended a hand for me to take. I stepped forward, my fingers sliding into his. "Laurel, this is my fiancée, Margot."

Laurel looked as if she were going to burst with joy. She quickly hugged me too, beaming at the both of us. "It's so, so wonderful to meet you. Both of you. I can't believe it," she said, shaking her head. "My baby brother shows up out of the blue. And he's brought a gorgeous fiancée with him."

I blushed hard at all of her gushing. "It's truly an honor to meet you, Laurel."

"Mommy?" the little girl called from the fence, her little face showing through the white slats.

"Just a few minutes sweetie," she called back. Suddenly, she seemed a little bit nervous. As excited as she was to be reunited with her brother, introducing this stranger to her children was a different aspect. "Go back and play with Charlie."

Laurel was once again beaming as she looked back at Nathaniel. "Tell me," she said, "where you've been. What you're doing now."

Nathaniel took a deep breath, and I could tell, he didn't want to recount the past too much. But this was part of their history, and that was what was needed. To fill in the blanks since the last time they saw each other.

So, he gave her a very brief brush over of what happened since he was three years old. How he'd bounced between foster homes, and then group homes. He told her how he'd gotten into some trouble when he was a kid and had to "deal with the consequences." When she gave an understanding nod, I wondered what trouble she might have gotten into as well.

"Then I realized that I needed to turn my life around or it was going to be real jail time or death, eventually,"

Nathaniel said. "So, I worked really hard and got good grades. I got a full ride scholarship to Alderidge University."

"Alderidge?" Laurel asked, stunned. "That's…that's one of the hardest universities in the area. And…only thirty minutes away."

Nathaniel nodded. "I've graduated, as of last month. But we still live there, in Harrington."

Once more, Laurel's eyes filled with happy tears. "I can't believe it. My baby brother has only been thirty minutes away, for years!"

Nathaniel let out a disbelieving laugh, shaking his head.

"And what do you do now?" she asked, so excited it was nearly contagious.

Nathaniel glanced at me, and anxiety hitched in my throat.

We hadn't discussed this, because, really, there hadn't been time. How much would we tell her? We hadn't had a chance to test her yet, though if Nathaniel had mage blood, it seemed nearly impossible that Laurel did not.

But as we looked back at the house, at those children playing in the yard, I had my own hope for what Nathaniel would say.

"We run a boarding school," Nathaniel said. "For lost youth who need guidance."

I had to work to contain my snort. Because it was the truth in the most stretched way possible.

"Really?" Laurel asked, obviously impressed. "You graduate college and immediately run your own school? I never would have guessed it was in our Nightingale blood."

Both of us simply smiled. Because she truly had no idea.

"What about you?" I asked. "Tell us about yourself."

Laurel smiled and glanced back at her children. They played happily with their toys in the yard. "My story was pretty similar to yours, Nathaniel. Bounced around a lot. Got into a little bit of trouble. But they gave me one more chance in a foster home when I was sixteen."

She blushed, and I wished I could see what she saw, really understand what she'd gone through.

"I was placed with the Sanders family," she said. "They had two teenagers of their own, older than me. And they were fostering two other teenagers besides me. They were the best people I'd ever met. I didn't feel like I had to be angry all the time anymore with them. I felt… safe for the first time ever. They loved me and I loved them."

I could see it shining in her eyes how much she meant the words. "They let me live with them until I was twenty-one, and that's when I met Raymond. They helped me plan and pay for the wedding and everything. We've been married for five years now."

So she was twenty-six. Three years older than Nathaniel.

She looked over her shoulder again. "That's Wendy. She's four. And Charlie, who is two."

"They're adorable," Nathaniel said admiringly.

"How does it feel to suddenly find out you're an uncle?" Laurel asked with a laugh.

Nathaniel laughed as well. "Good. Maybe a little overwhelming. But it's..." He shook his head, at a loss for words again. I could only imagine the tidal wave of emotions he was experiencing.

I squeezed his hand a little tighter.

"Raymond is still at work," she said. "But he would love to meet you. He's a good guy."

"I'd be honored to meet them all," Nathaniel said, but his tone did communicate that maybe he needed to take this one step at a time.

"I need to go take dinner out of the oven and check on the rest of the food," Laurel said, departure and goodbye in her eyes. "But can we maybe, go out for dinner next week? Keep getting to know each other?"

"I'd really like that," Nathaniel said with a nod and a hopeful smile.

She smiled too and they exchanged phone numbers. And then they both said a hesitant and hopeful goodbye.

I climbed into the driver's seat, and Nathaniel dropped into his, staring quietly ahead.

"You okay?" I asked, worried.

And slowly, a smile spread on Nathaniel's face. It was the happiest I'd seen him since our engagement. "I'm amazing. That was... I couldn't have asked for anything better. Thank you for coming with me, Margot. And for encouraging me to look for my family. This feeling of closure...it's really wonderful."

I leaned across the center and pressed my lips to his. "You always had it in you. And I'm really happy for you."

I put the car into drive, and we pulled down the road.

"I don't think I'm going to tell her," Nathaniel said after a quiet moment of thought. "Even if she is a mage, and even if she isn't locked. With those two kids... She already has her own life, and she seems happy. Why would I go and throw so many complications into it when she's already living such a great life?"

I wasn't sure if it was the right move or not. People must make their own decisions. But he was also well aware of all the hardship that came with the knowledge that we had.

You protect the ones you love.

So I trusted that he was making the right decision.

I reached across and took his hand. He lifted the back of my hand to his lips and pressed a kiss there. And I could just feel it. A new peace in him that he'd never had before.

And I loved him still the same.

CHAPTER THIRTEEN

I paced nervously in the kitchen, trying to count the minutes since Nathaniel left. It had been nearly an hour and a half. They should be back any minute.

"Why are you so damn nervous?" Mary-Beth asked as she pulled the plates from the cupboard and went to set the four of them on the massive table.

"Have you never met Borden?" I asked as I looked outside at the skies. There was a gray haze in the sky to the north, but it wasn't a full-on storm. "His emotions can cause volatile weather. His father, who cut him off, just died. You don't expect a little fall out from that?"

Mary-Beth shrugged and leaned against the counter. "I guess I haven't thought about it. Sometimes I think you were meant to have two soul mates. No one reads him quite like you do, Margot."

I stopped in my tracks at that and my eyes ripped to her.

"Don't say that," I said around a thick throat.

She shrugged again. "Sorry. It's just kind of true. It's obvious he's in love with you. And even though you and Nathaniel were clearly made for each other like no one in the history of the planet, you and Borden have this…jive about you. I'm just saying." She held her hands up in surrender.

"Can we please not talk about it?" I said, and with my words, I confirmed everything she had just said, without meaning to. "You're not making things any easier. We just…need to be supportive of him, whatever happened."

Just then, I heard the garage opening and then the sound of the car as it pulled in.

My mouth felt dry and once more, I glanced outside. So far, the gray haze in the sky stayed further north.

That was a good sign.

The door opened, and I heard their footsteps. They stepped around the corner, and my eyes landed on Nathaniel, and then Borden.

"Welcome home," I said, offering Borden a cautious smile.

He gave me a small, ingenuine one in return.

"Dinner's ready. Hope everyone is hungry."

I grabbed one pot and carried it to the table, followed

by Mary-Beth and Nathaniel with the rest of the food. We set it all on the table, and we all sat down together.

It had been awkward, but I'd asked all of the students to make themselves scarce tonight. They'd all eaten an early dinner and headed to their bedrooms, or out into town, or to the beach.

Tonight, it just needed to be the four of us, who were all in this together originally.

"How was your flight?" I asked in mindless conversation as I served my food onto my plate.

"Fine," Borden said with the tiniest of huffs, which told me that he knew exactly what I was doing.

We finished dishing up. Borden grabbed his fork and knife, but just sat there, staring at a blank space on the table.

"My father knew he was going to die, that's why he finally asked to see me," he said, diving right into it, because he was never one to beat around the bush. "He didn't seem particularly thrilled when I walked into his room, but he didn't change his mind and throw me out."

Borden stabbed his fork into his food and cut off a bite. He stuffed it into his mouth and chewed with vigor. Meanwhile, the rest of us sat there without touching our food. Because the clouds had moved further south to hover out over the ocean.

"He interrogated me," Borden continued when he finished swallowing his bite. "Wanted to know what I'd accomplished since I left the Society Boys, since I got myself kicked out of school."

Just one more tie. Borden and I had both wanted to get revenge on the Society Boys that night. We'd done something reckless together. We'd gotten expelled from the university, together.

"I didn't want to tell him anything," Borden said. "I had nothing to prove to him. But how do you not grant a dying man his last question?" He took a moment then, dragging in deep breaths. The clouds above the sea grew a little darker, but I heard no thunder. "I told him about my dealings in the stock market. I told him that I had helped found a boarding school. I told him the truth in the ways he wanted to hear it."

I wasn't sure what that meant, but I trusted Borden. He wouldn't say anything that would put us at risk.

"He asked me if it was worth it, leaving the Society for my new friends." Finally, Borden's eyes rose. First, he met Nathaniel's eyes. Then Mary-Beth's. And finally, mine. "I told him that I would have betrayed the Society Boys for anything. I would have used them for gain, and I would have slept like a baby after doing it. I told him that I would die for you all, and I meant every word."

It was there in his eyes, the truth of that statement. He might have been struggling, might have needed his space, because of me. But he meant what he said.

"In the end, he still cut me out of his business, good riddance. I wanted no part of it. But he…" Borden swallowed once, his eyes falling to the table again. "He revoked his disownment. Said he respected my loyalty to my friends and my ability to choose my own path. He put me back in the will."

He didn't have to say it for us to know what that meant. Once more, Borden was exceptionally wealthy.

He'd always been rich. He was going to do just fine on his own. He didn't need to live in this house as a charity case. He could easily go buy his own.

But now he had millions and millions.

He was the descendant of actual royalty, after all.

"I tested him, just an hour before he died," Borden said, looking down at his food. "My father was a mage. He wasn't locked."

The breath hitched in my throat and my grip on my fork tightened.

"My sister, Chloe, is also a mage," Borden said. He took one deep breath, and it looked like relief. "She, however, is locked."

There was a huge lump in my throat and I did my best to swallow around it. "Poppy called. She was back in Scotland. She got to visit her family. Her brother, the one that is a doctor, he's locked as well."

"Fifty percent," Mary-Beth said with a nod. "The Lock of Sandris."

Borden nodded as well. "My mother was quiet. Distant. But she did give me a hug before I left. She asked me to come back for Thanksgiving this year."

I reached over and laid my hand on Borden's. "That's wonderful."

His eyes didn't rise to meet mine, but he gave a tiny, tight-lipped smile and nodded.

This. This was what family was really about. Because it was heavy and dark, and dinner was not particularly comfortable. But none of us would have chosen to be anywhere else. We would be here, holding each other up during the hard times. No matter what.

CHAPTER FOURTEEN

Classes were over and I was digging through a closet, looking for the box of journals I knew were in there somewhere. The fact that I had yet to read through Mare McGregor's journal was eating away at me. In reality, I was terrified of it after Mary-Beth and I had that vision in Salem. Seeing her hanged to death was horrific. I was not anxious to read her words and go through any similar experiences.

But the guilt was now eating at me.

I moved one box and grabbed the next when the lid fell off.

Inside, there was an odd assortment of things Borden and I had stolen from a Hexenhaus in Germany from a very sweet man named Otto.

There were half a dozen crystals inside. A small human skull. A ball of yarn. A pair of wooden shoes.

And carefully rolled with a rubber band around it, a map.

Something sparked through my entire body when my eyes landed on the map.

Each of these random items had made our wands light up in that little shop in Germany, meaning they held some kind of magical property. We'd had so much on our plates and were concentrating on the books that we hadn't bothered to learn what these could do yet.

But the map…

I snatched it from the box and pulled the rubber band off. There, in the hallway, I rolled the map out on the floor.

It was a map of the entire world. It wasn't accurate by modern standards, but generally, the whole globe was there.

"Borden!" I called out without thinking. I stood, holding the map in front of me.

Borden barreled out of his bedroom instantly, looking for the source of danger. Electricity sparked around his hands, ready to maim or kill.

I looked up at him, ignoring his ready-for-battle state. "The map! We found a map at Hexenhaus! I…" I shook my head in disbelief. "I can't believe I forgot about it. What if-"

"We can use it to make the tracking spell work?" he finished for me, his eyes growing wider as he walked to my side and looked down at the map.

It was ordinary looking. Old. But there were no markings on it, no Xs showing where treasure might be hidden.

"What's going on?" Nathaniel called from down below.

I leaned over the railing. "Hurry up here. Mary-Beth!"

Multiple heads were popping out of their rooms now, but I ignored them all as I headed up the spiral staircase for my office, taking them two at a time. Borden followed right on my heels.

I laid the map flat on my desk, putting random books and an empty cup on the corners to keep it from curling back in on itself. I looked up at the globe standing in the corner with its flashing lights that made no sense.

Nathaniel walked into the office, followed immediately by Mary-Beth.

"When Borden and I were in Germany, we went to Hexenhaus, that's where we got all those German books," I explained in a blurt. "But we also found a bunch of random objects that tested as magical. This map was one of those things."

"We're trying to work magic on an ordinary object," Borden thought out loud. "But maybe this will make the difference."

"Only one way to find out," Mary-Beth said. "What are we waiting for?"

Nathaniel turned and grabbed the hairbrush that was

sitting on a shelf, the one that had belonged to Olin. He set it down in the center of the map. Mary-Beth turned out the lights and Borden grabbed the candles, setting them around the room and lighting them.

We each grabbed hands and closed our eyes.

"Let he who is lost be revealed," we each said. "Show us he who must be brought to justice."

The request and the reason. In our research, what little we found, we had decided that there needed to be two parts. The words were simple and quick, despite them taking us weeks to decide upon.

But as we opened our eyes, each of our mouths hung open in awe.

The hairbrush was standing on end on the map, balanced perfectly on its narrow point.

It was pointed in England. On a location just over the border from Whales.

There were no multiple blinking lights. There was nothing else to the map.

Just the brush, used and owned by Olin, still containing strands of his hair, pointing directly to one place on the map.

"Looks like we've found him," Nathaniel said, the words filled with awe.

"Now what?" Mary-Beth asked. "We jump on a flight and walk around with this map and brush like a bunch of lunatics?"

Borden set something down on the map in front of

us, just to the side of the floating brush.

It was a worn leather-bound book. It rested there, familiar and heavy as the entire world.

The portal book.

A dark hollow pit opened in my stomach the moment I laid eyes on it. They rose to look at Borden.

"Olin mastered it," Borden said, his voice quiet and low. "We didn't even know he had touched the book and he mastered it. It's possible."

"It's also possible to get yourself horribly lost for years and years," I said, my words hard, even through the thickness in my throat. "We've tried a lot of magic so far, Borden. And this is the only magic that has brought about true sorrow in our lives."

I shook my head.

"But it is possible, Margot." I could see the acknowledgement in Borden's eyes. It was accompanied by apology. But also desperation. "Can you imagine? If we could master portal magic? It would change so much. Think how much more quickly we could expand this? How many more people we could test? How many books we could find."

I *had* imagined it. This portal book had always been there in the back of my mind, since the moment we realized what it was in a small, crowded hotel room in Scotland. I knew what it could mean for us and the academy and our entire race.

"My mother made one small mistake. Got distracted

for just a moment. Didn't understand it just enough. And she got stuck in a jungle in China for years. She ended up being sold as a magical slave for years. We thought she was dead. And she plain and simply got lucky that she was able to come up with a combination that brought her home."

Nathaniel reached across the desk and grabbed the portal book. He set it back on a shelf. "Margot is right. We can't take the risk. Not yet. Maybe someday when we've mastered things more. Maybe someday when we can have it translated with precise confidence. But not yet."

Borden looked at us with darkness, but I could see, he knew. Was he really ready to take the risk? He understood some Mandarin, but not enough.

He knew what his likely fate would be if he opened that book and performed the magic within.

"So we head to England?" Mary-Beth asked. "We book flights, and then, what? Go at him with all the battle magic we've been practicing?"

She was being sarcastic. And in that moment, I realized how much we were still children.

This was our plan, what we'd declared had to happen. That we needed to take Olin out before he endangered our kind all over again. We knew we were going to have to deal with him for the past month.

But what had we been doing to prepare for it? What spells had we learned that would help us fight against him, short of being able to knock him out or use telekinesis to hurt him with objects we could throw at him with our minds?

Not a single one of us had truly grasped the reality of what it would take to solve this problem that put us in danger.

We were talking about war. About bloodshed. About probable death.

Nathaniel let out a curse, and I knew he was having the same realizations I was. He ran a hand over his face slowly and then crossed his arms over his chest. "We need to strike as soon as possible, because he's killed twice now, and it seems likely he'll do it again. But we have to face the reality that we are not prepared to go to war with him."

"We spend the next week preparing specifically to fight," Borden concluded. "We involve the students. We practice every bit of battle magic we can get our hands on."

My stomach knotted in dread.

This was what I didn't want to involve them in. I didn't want Aleem and Alexandra and Marie and my mother mixed up with Olin.

But we couldn't do this alone. Not fast enough.

"You all know what books you've studied," I said as I took a breath in, resolving myself that I was going to have to do what I never wanted to do. "Grab anything that might be useful. We have research to do, and not very long to do it."

CHAPTER FIFTEEN

There was something about the energy in the house. It was quiet, but there was this buzz humming through the entire space. The synergy of something about to happen. Danger and sparks of adrenaline hung in the very near future and we were all alert and alive with it.

Everyone was awake and spread throughout the house. Marie, Julie, Abigale and Alexandra were spread out at the dining table, piles of books around them with little tabs of paper stuck out of them. John and Dorian stood in the kitchen with Peter, hunched over yet another pile of books.

Mom and Dad were curled up on the couch together, each of them flying through book after book.

Mary-Beth and Poppy were sitting on the floor, their backs pressed against the couch. Borden paced back and forth in front of the big windows, reading furiously.

We were all spread out, every single one of us doing our part to search for battle magic and anything that might help us.

Nathaniel and I were sitting on the floor, leaning against the wall that opened into the library, books and pages of notes spread before us.

As wary as I had been to involve all of them, I had to admit, this felt amazing. This felt possible. With this many minds focused on the same things, it felt as if we could actually do this. Little conversations cropped up between the different groups. They bounced ideas, shared their findings.

It was nearing two in the morning, but no one showed any signs of being tired.

I looked down at the list in my lap and read through it one more time.

Fire starting
Transfiguring weapons
Invisibility
Knock out

Pathetic. This wasn't near enough. After thinking through every book we had and everything we'd yet come across, this was all I found.

I rubbed my fingertips into my temples and let out a sigh.

Automatically, Nathaniel reached out a hand and rubbed it over my back. "We can do this," he said quietly.

"I know," I said, sitting up straighter and reaching out

for another book. "This is just one of those times that I'm woefully reminded that we've been doing this for less than two years. And we're starting from scratch, essentially."

Nathaniel extended a hand, as if putting everyone around us on display. "But at least we're not alone."

Just then, Alexandra sat straighter. "I've got something here. It's some kind of…clap. It's written in terrible handwriting. But it sounds like you use certain hand motions, and then when directed, it emits this powerful wave from the clap. Enough to knock people out or knock them off their feet."

"Excellent," Nathaniel said as he climbed off the floor and went to go look over her shoulder. That's when I knew he'd needed a breakthrough just as much as I did. He wasn't one to hover.

"This one talks about what they call a fear whisper," Borden said, pausing in his pacing. "It doesn't sound easy. It talks about tapping into your own worst fears and letting them engulf you. But you can take that fear and direct it at your enemy. Supposedly, it can be enough to completely incapacitate someone. They can't think clearly and sometimes, they can't even move."

"That sounds awful," I said, imagining it. What was my greatest fear? And how did I feel about inflicting that upon someone else in such a strong way that it incapacitated them?

"But immensely effective, possibly," Borden said without even looking up.

"I have something here," Aleem said. "They refer to it as 'the cover of darkness.' It's not particularly clear what it does exactly, but it makes it so your enemies and those on your side can't see one another. Perhaps it's a literal cloud."

As slow as all of this felt, we were gaining knowledge every day. Our translations were slowly coming back. Several of the Swiss ones and a handful of the German ones had been waiting for our review. With everything going on, we hardly had time to go through them.

And now that discovery was being made by students with weeks or months of training.

"I like the sound of that one," Thomas said. "It's hard for your enemy to strike against you if they can't see you."

"Maybe we could duplicate the magic from the invisibility book," Mary-Beth pointed out. "We've physically touched it, but no one has bothered to translate it yet. Maybe it has instructions on how to replicate it."

I nodded in agreement.

Borden snapped his book closed. "I think that no matter what we find, we all need to cloak a weapon. Like my walking staff. Like Margot's pearls."

I reached up and hooked a finger around them. I'd worn them every day since Olin tried to kill me.

"You want us walking in there with swords and daggers?" Dorian asked with a raised eyebrow.

"Olin knows old magic and old history," Borden said as he stood with the book clutched behind his back. "He's lied about countless things. Who knows if he ever learned to lock magic like Sandris and his followers? It goes against everything he's trying to accomplish, but it is massively effective against an enemy who is a mage, fighting back with magic. If any of us are in battle and were to lose our connection with magic, I think it's important for us to still be able to defend ourselves."

I tried to gauge everyone's reactions to this. Some were pale and I wondered if they were second guessing their willingness to fight. Others nodded in agreement. Some were simply stony faced.

"I think that's an excellent place to start, in the morning," Nathaniel said. "You've all done a tremendous amount of work. I feel confident we will make the strides necessary this week to deal with Olin. Classes will be combined this week, first and second semester students all together. We're all learning new things this week. Let's get some rest. We'll start fresh in the morning."

And there the tiredness was. There were stretches and yawns. Others groggily got to their feet and said goodnight as they slipped up the stairs to their bedrooms.

"It's late," I said to my parents as I crossed to their side. "And you'll be back in the morning. There are several empty bedrooms upstairs. Why don't you just stay here tonight?"

Mom and Dad glanced at each other, having a silent conversation, but Mom smiled. "Thanks, sweetie. We'll see you in the morning."

It felt…good, and weird, to watch my parents walking up the stairs in my home to stay the night. But I was so grateful for this house and everything it meant for us.

Nathaniel quickly took Khan back outside to potty one last time, and then the three of us headed into our bedroom. Khan jumped up onto the bed and curled up at the foot of it.

"You know that's going to be a problem when he's as big as you are, right?" I pointed out while I brushed my teeth.

Nathaniel sat on the edge of the bed and rubbed behind his puppy's ears. "I know. But how can I let him be lonely on the floor with those eyes?"

I chuckled and spit in the sink, rinsing my mouth out. I changed into pajamas and crawled up onto the bed.

I scratched behind Khan's ears and he licked my hand happily before lying his head down on the bed. The poor pup was exhausted.

And I had to admit as I crawled into the covers, that I didn't mind him in our bed.

For now.

Nathaniel flicked the light off in the bathroom when he was done and crawled into the bed. He wrapped an arm around my waist and slid right up behind me, every surface of his body lining up with mine.

Softly, he pressed a kiss to the back of my neck, and I smiled in the dark.

"Good night, Margot," he whispered.

"Good night," I said back, and let sleep drag me down into oblivion.

The morning didn't start with magic, but a shopping trip.

It wasn't like we had a bunch of weapons lying around Nightingale Academy, so out into the world everyone went.

They all came back with an assortment of weapons, several of them surprising, several of them very underwhelming.

I smiled at Nathaniel's. Leave it to a history buff to come back with a morning star, which was a three-foot-long shaft with an iron ball attached to the end of it. Deadly metal spikes jutted out from the ball, vicious and arcane.

It had been months since Borden and I had cloaked our weapons, and even when we did it, it hadn't been smooth or easy. So we spent the entire morning practicing right along with our students.

It required real commitment, real intent that you had to defend yourself and hurt another, to trigger the shift from ordinary object back to weapon. Thomas nearly took Peter's head off as his weapon shifted from a baseball cap back into a battle axe.

Poor John got a thick cut down his chest when Marie shifted a necklace back into a whip. I pulled him aside and used healing magic to close the wound up and sent him off to go shower the blood off and change.

Borden walked among the students, checking their work, all the while carrying a replica of my grandfather's snake-headed black cane. He easily shifted it back and forth between the staff and the sword, the most fluid of all of us by a long way.

By lunch, we felt we had enough of a handle to break to eat, and immediately move on to the next topic.

The knockout magic I'd accidentally performed on Borden once was one that he and I had practiced on each other until we'd mastered it. It wasn't one I was anxious to teach the students, but it was exceptionally effective, so long as you could touch your enemy.

And the only way for them to practice, was on each other.

It was telling of their personalities, who volunteered to be knocked out first and who was very anxious to try knocking someone out first. Immediately, it was Nathaniel, Peter, Abigail, and Dorian lying on the ground, knocked out and having the best sleep of their life on the floor for a good thirty minutes.

Then it switched. Aleem, however, had to sit this one out. Any magic that involved touching skin to skin was a no-go for him. We couldn't risk any kind of accident.

Back and forth, we practiced the magic, one group knocking out the other, Borden and I instructing in ways they could control, making the amounts of time shorter and shorter. I remembered a time last year when he and I practiced on each other, just the two of us in my father's house. We had all the time in the world because we'd been expelled from school.

Now here we were, with no school time frame on us, other than our own, but with time quickly running out, because we needed to take care of a man who would expose us to the world. A man who had killed because they wouldn't agree to do what he wanted.

After dinner, we moved on to the clap that Alexandra had found in the book.

I was grateful that the property the academy sat upon was two entire acres. That gave us one hundred yards of quiet beach. Not that no one might wander along. But it was less likely down this far among the private residences. Dad kept an eye out, being kept company by Mary-Beth, while we all practiced on the beach so that we didn't destroy the house.

The clap was performed fairly easily. With a series of hand motions, it built up this…energy in your hands. It was so overwhelming that I desperately *wanted* to release it.

Borden volunteered to be the first target. I'd stood on the beach in the fading light and muttered over and over to myself that I wouldn't hurt him.

I directed my gaze at him.

And I clapped my hands together, pointing them in his direction.

I could actually see the air ripple out in front of my hands. Like waves on the water, they got bigger and bigger. Sand sprayed out, the grasses on the shoreline laid over sideways.

And Borden blasted out backward away from us. He was lifted off his feet and flew back, before landing on his back in the sand, a good thirty feet back from where he had been standing.

"Borden!" I called out as I sprinted across the sand toward him. Nathaniel was right by my side and reached Borden first, dropping to his side in the sand.

"You alright?" Nathaniel asked, looking Borden over for signs of damage.

Borden groaned as he sat up, sand pouring off of him. He shook his head and looked up at the two of us. "I think I like this one. Just maybe not from this end."

I let out a laugh in relief, and we both extended a hand down to help Borden climb to his feet.

For the next two hours, long after the sun sank below the city behind us, we stayed on that beach and practiced the clap. Each of us got to be the victim once. It was like being punched in the entire torso before being blasted back by a huge force of wind. More than one of us had the wind knocked from our lungs upon the harsh landing and had to lay there until we could catch our breath once more.

But by the end of the day, everyone had mastered the clap. Everyone could knock someone out by just a touch and control the length of time they would stay out for. And everyone could cloak a weapon and bring it back, ready to defend or fight.

I climbed into bed thinking that just maybe we could do this.

CHAPTER SIXTEEN

Considering we were doing all of this because of him, it shouldn't have been a surprise that I dreamt of Olin that night.

He was following me through the house, watching everything I was working on with the students. He lurked in the corners, watching from the shadows. In the dream, I was hiding everything from him by turning my back and whispering quietly. Yet I did nothing to deal with him or make him leave.

I woke up with a chill running down my spine and the feeling that he was watching me.

Yet the map still said he was in England.

We quickly reviewed everything we had learned the day before. There were a few stumbling blocks, but within an hour, everyone had it under control again.

We moved on to the fear whisper.

I didn't want to practice this one. I didn't like the idea of it. But we needed everything in our arsenal that we could find.

Tap into your deepest fears, the book had said. *Let it consume you.*

We all sat in the living room, circled up, our eyes closed. We were each searching our souls for what our deepest fear was.

What was mine? I didn't think it was anything trivially physical like spiders or heights. I thought of what had caused me fear before.

Not knowing what had happened to my mother.

Watching the spiral of grief my father went into for a few months following her disappearance.

Watching the Society Boys try to drown Nathaniel.

The vision of Mare McGregor's hanging in Salem.

Thinking I'd exposed Borden and I in Germany when I'd unknowingly grabbed the invisibility book in public.

Realizing who Olin really was.

Thinking I was going to die at his hand when it was wrapped around my throat.

And then all of my biggest fearful moments in my past started to fuse together as my imagination took hold.

It was my mother at Olin's hands. It was Mary-Beth being drowned by the Society Boy's hands. It was Nathaniel and Julie and Thomas and Alexandra hanging in those trees in Salem.

And I realized what my greatest fear was then.

It was my loved ones getting hurt or exposed.

That was my greatest fear of all.

"I'm ready," I said without meaning to.

"Me as well," Nathaniel said.

We shifted and sat in front of each other, cross legged on the floor.

My heart was thundering in my chest, hardly able to be contained.

I didn't want to do this. But I knew we had to.

"Go ahead," Nathaniel said, lifting his chin and nodding. "You first."

I knew he was going to volunteer to be the first victim before he did it. I'd been preparing myself mentally for it. This was the man I loved more than anything, and I was going to inflict my fear upon him.

I took a deep breath. I closed my eyes.

I imagined all the most horrible things I could happening to those I loved. I let them race through me, fill every single corner of my mind. A cold sweat broke out on my palms and my upper lip. My breathing increased and I started to feel sick.

It washed through me, threatening to crush me.

But then, I opened my eyes. It was Nathaniel sitting before me. But mentally, I imagined Olin and no one else.

"Feel my fear," I said flatly.

It was a visceral, physical sensation. The fear ripped up from every corner of my body. Like a gush of a geyser, it rippled up and out of me, blasting forward, leaving me feeling a million pounds lighter as it left my body.

I couldn't see anything physically moving through the air, but I saw the moment it hit Nathaniel. His shoulders caved inward as he stumbled back just slightly. He sucked in a horrific, terrified breath and his eyes doubled in size. He sucked in another breath, and another. His hands rose to his throat, and he let out a terrified scream as he tipped backward onto his back. It arched off the floor and he started pushing himself farther away from me as he continued yelling in complete terror.

"Nathaniel!" I yelled as I got up and scrambled to his side.

He looked at me with absolute horror and continued to try to get away from me.

I felt completely sick and horrified. I'd done this to him. I'd inflicted this on him, and now he had lost his mind in panic.

A slew of curse words slipped from my mouth as my hands hovered over him, completely unsure of how to fix this or how to make it end.

A feral cry ripped up Nathaniel's throat and he twisted, hard, on the floor. Blood red veins crept into his eyes. He twisted onto his stomach, and his hands clawed at the floor as he tried to drag himself away from me.

Wildly, I looked back for help.

But it was just students who stared at us with their own terror, not knowing what to do.

It was Borden who got up and crossed to Nathaniel. With one touch, he knocked him out, and instantly, his terrified cries were silenced, and he lay still.

Everyone was voiceless for a very long moment. My entire body was shaking with the severity of what I'd just done to Nathaniel. When my stomach rolled, I lurched to my feet and made for the bathroom.

I threw up just as I clutched the toilet.

There were times that magic was wonderful and spectacular. It still amazed me, and I loved all our discoveries.

But there were ugly sides to magic. There were reasons people feared it. Not every mage was good. Not everything we could perform was for the general good. There were tricks and spells I wished didn't exist. There were books and powers that should be erased from the Earth.

I wished I had never done that to Nathaniel. I wished I could bleach the image of his terrified eyes from my mind.

But I also knew how effective this would be used against an enemy.

I spat in the toilet, flushed, and then rinsed my mouth in the sink.

I was still shaking horribly from head to toe. I felt exhausted and strung out.

I walked out of the bathroom to everyone staring at me. I didn't meet any of their eyes.

I tapped into my telekinesis and latched onto Nathaniel. I lifted him into the air and guided him to our bedroom.

Without a word, I followed in after him, and shut the door behind me.

Gently, I rested Nathaniel on our bed.

I hated doing that to him. I hated seeing him lying there limp and unresponsive.

Over and over, his terrified eyes flashed in my mind.

I knew I should be out in the living room, reassuring the students and making decisions on whether we should continue practicing the fear whisper. I was in charge. I needed to show confidence and make it seem as if I knew what I was doing.

But right now, I was checked out.

I was human. And the love of my life was unconscious because of something I did to him.

I crawled up into the bed beside him. I carefully situated the pillow beneath his head. Laid his arms out in a comfortable position. I pulled his shoes off. And then I curled up into his side.

I didn't know how long Borden had intended to knock Nathaniel out for. But I was determined that I would be here when he woke up, so I laid beside him, for however long it took.

. . .

His hand twitched, tightening on my side, his fingers gripping my hip. I turned my head toward him, watching as his brows furrowed, a deep V forming between them. He twisted his head, his chin digging hard into the pillow.

And then his eyes flew open, and with a startled gasp, he flinched away from me.

"It's just me," I said quickly, bringing my hand to the side of his face. Nathaniel instantly calmed the moment my skin came into contact with his. With a deep breath, he brought his hand up to mine, covering my skin with his own.

"What happened?" he asked, confused.

A knot formed in my throat and my eyes dropped away from his. My words seemed to be stuck in my throat. "I...I was practicing the fear whisper. It was... very effective. You...took the full brunt of it. Borden had to knock you out to make it stop."

Nathaniel was quiet for a moment, and warily, I looked back up at him. His gaze was fixed on the ceiling, but I could see him mulling it all over.

"It *was* very effective," he said, ever logical and progressive. "I...the fear was incredible. Absolute horror."

Finally, he looked at me and seemed to realize that something was wrong. "Oh, Margot," he said as he circled his arms around me. "I am not angry. You did what needed to be done. You did it astoundingly. It was horrific, truly. But these are the risks we take in learning new things."

I shook my head, unable to look at him again. "You didn't see it from my end. You didn't see the look in your eyes. The fear when you looked at me…" I shook my head again, recalling every horrifying moment of it. "I won't ever do the fear whisper on one of our own again."

His grip on me tightened and he pulled me in tight. Gently, he pressed his lips to my forehead. "I'm so sorry," he said softly. Somehow, he always knew the words to calm my heart. "We won't ever do it in this house again. I promise. No fear inflicting upon one another."

I burrowed into his chest and nodded, at a loss for words, because yet again, the scene of him writhing on the floor in terror was playing in my mind.

"How are the others?" he asked. "They have to be so horrified."

"I don't know," I muttered. "I…I kind of checked out after what happened. I brought you in here, and we stayed here."

Once more, he kissed my forehead. He sat up, looking down at me. Gently, he caressed the side of my face. "I'm going to go check on them."

I shook my head. "I…I can't. Not today, Nathaniel."

He shook his head as well. "Don't. You stay here. Do what you need. I'll take care of it."

I swallowed, my throat still feeling tight. But I nodded. He leaned forward, kissing me softly, and in it there were a thousand promises. That he would take care of me. In these moments where I just…couldn't, he would do it for me. He would always pave the way.

I watched him as he walked out the door and gently closed it behind him.

I rolled onto my side and curled up into myself. Out in the living room, I could hear Nathaniel softly speaking. I couldn't hear all of his words, but generally, he told them that he was okay. He told the students that he didn't want anyone practicing it on one of our own. They were to tap into what their greatest fears were, and to remember how I had done it, and if they thought it would be effective in defending themselves, they were to use it.

The fear whisper hadn't been hard. Once I'd tapped into my fears, it was literally a matter of fixing my gaze and saying three words. It wouldn't take practice.

Like the professor he was, Nathaniel moved onto the next thing.

I couldn't even concentrate to find out what it was.

I got up and went into the bathroom. I filled up the bathtub, dumped way too much bubble bath in, and climbed inside.

I forced myself to put every ounce of magic out of my mind. I focused on what was "normal." I was getting married in just a few weeks. I got to spend the rest of my life with a man I admired more than anyone, someone I trusted and loved.

I lived in a fantastic home that had been such a huge blessing.

I had two wonderful parents who loved me, who were together, and who supported me in everything I did.

I had friends who would do anything for me, and I would in return.

In the hard moments, I had to ground myself like this. I had to return to being a woman. A person. I had to find gratitude when the circumstances surrounding me felt crushingly overwhelming.

I hadn't even realized how long I'd been in my room until I finally stepped from the bath, pulled on pajamas and crawled into bed—and it was already getting dark outside.

There was a soft knock at the door. She didn't wait for me to call her in before Mary-Beth walked in through.

She held two plates of food, one balanced on each hand. "I thought maybe you could use some refueling."

Instantly, my stomach growled ravenously. "Sometimes I think you're actually a mind reader."

She smiled and made her way across the bedroom to come sit on my bed. She handed me one of the plates.

"Peter's turn to cook?" I guessed as I looked down at the delicious food on the plate. He really was a spectacular cook.

"Of course," she said. She curled her feet in front of her, sitting cross legged. "So," she said as she forked some potatoes into her mouth. "Today sucked."

"It truly wasn't my favorite," I said, raising my eyebrows as I stabbed my own food and ate it.

"You're really the bravest person I know," she said as her eyes rose to meet mine. "Do you know that?"

I slowed in my chewing, looking at my best friend.

Mary-Beth nodded and took another bite, not bothering to swallow it before she started speaking again. "It's true. I tend to be all talk and act as if nothing ever bothers me. But what does that really accomplish? You…" She shook her head and stirred her food with her fork. "You're always charging right in and you hardly ever even hesitate. You're experimenting with magic with your freaking life, every single day, and I don't think you ever think about that. No mentor, no sage old man who had a trainer before that. It's just you. And you're always jumping right in."

My throat felt thick again, but for an entirely different reason. "Mary-Beth, I-"

"I don't know that I could do it the same," she said, cutting me off as she looked at me again. "What you do. If I wasn't locked, I'm not sure I wouldn't be scared to try new things all the time. But you…you don't even question it. Sometimes it's too late, like today, and I get reminders that you are, in fact, human. But I hope you love that about yourself. How fearless you really are."

Emotions sprang into my eyes. My throat tightened further, and my entire chest swelled with love and gratitude.

I set my plate aside and pulled her into a hug. I didn't say anything for a long time, just held her. She set her own plate to the side and wrapped her arms around me in return. And we just held each other like that. We were two sisters who loved and supported each other, even though in most ways, we were nothing alike.

But we were here to cheer each other along. Two women who would support each other to the very end, no matter how the world tried to wear us down.

"You're the best," I said with emotion cracking my words.

"Takes one to know one," she said in a classic Mary-Beth response.

I pressed a quick kiss to her cheek and let her go, taking an emotional sniff and wiping at my eyes.

"So, tell me," Mary-Beth said, moving on as she grabbed her food again. "Are you planning to go with classic white on your wedding night, or will it be straight to black for the night of finally doing the deed?"

I gaped at her, shocked…and entirely not, at the same time.

And she laughed at my blushing and I scolded her for being so brash.

But it was exactly what I needed to get my mind off the darkness of the day.

. . .

I DREAMT of Olin again that night. We were both sitting in the living room, him in one chair, me on the opposite couch. We stared at each other intensely. It was not the beginning of our conversation, but like all dreams, I was suddenly an actor in the middle of a scene.

"It's your own fault, you know," Olin said.

"For uncovering the truth?" I asked him.

"For being too curious," he responded. "Things would be entirely different for us if you hadn't learned about my past."

"How do you figure?" I asked. My frustration and anger were rising.

"Had you not figured out who I was, I would be studying with your students," he said as he crossed one leg over the other knee. "I could have had more time to make you understand. We could have collaborated. We could have come up with a plan, together. We wouldn't all be hiding in this house."

I shook my head. "Why do you need to be in the limelight, Olin? Why isn't life as it is enough for you?"

"Why do you not strive for more?" he turned it around with another question.

"I have enough," I answered honestly. "We find happiness in our current circumstances. I want what I have. I don't need the entire world looking at me."

Olin shook his head and I could see his own frustration building on his face. "Our people have been burned at the stake for centuries. Are you okay with them dying in vain?"

That thought gave me pause. Their deaths were not in vain. People are afraid. They do what they can to overcome that fear. The humans thought they were in danger from the mages. It went too far, and so many innocent people were accused. But people thought they were in danger. It was a horrific injustice, that they had died for being what they were because another group of people chose to target them.

"I believe there's more happiness in peace and safety," I said, even though for the first time, Olin got me to pause and consider.

He shook his head again. "You have so much potential, Margot. If I could only make you see."

And then the bed shifted. My eyes fluttered open to see Nathaniel getting up from the bed and heading to go get ready for the day.

But still, in the back of my mind, there was Olin, trying to put doubt in my head.

CHAPTER SEVENTEEN

"What's the plan, Margot?"

I stood beside my father, watching as Thomas blasted airwaves at Dorian. As Mom clapped her hands at Alexandra. While Aleem and Poppy practiced transforming their weapons into ordinary objects and then back again. John was casting a cloud of darkness around him and Peter.

Dad stood with his arms folded over his chest, glaring darkly at the students practicing in front of us.

"What do you mean?" I asked, noting that Abigale was struggling.

"I mean, the fact that you are planning to go to war with a mage who tried to kill you and who has now murdered two humans for not giving him what he wants. You may be one of the most capable people I've ever had the pleasure of knowing, but you could get yourself killed doing this."

I looked over at him, and for a moment, it was just me and him again. Worry for each other and too much unknown. Father and daughter, us against the world.

"It's going to be fourteen against one," I pointed out, marveling at that number. Once upon a time, it was just Nathaniel, and then just the two of us. "I think I like those odds."

Dad shook his head. "Still. None of you are combat trained. You've never had to attack someone before. Fighting has a way of making people freeze up."

"There isn't an alternative, Dad," I said. "Olin is hurting people, killing them, because he believes the way he does so strongly. As far as we know, there is no one else to go up against him. He's held on to this fight for two and a half centuries. He isn't just going to let it go."

Dad let out a hard breath and I could tell he still didn't like any of this. He pulled me into his arms and hugged me tight against him. "You're my only daughter," he said, resting his chin on the top of my head. "This is terrifying. What you do. Every single day. You're always at risk. And you're doing amazing things. I just can't imagine how life would be if anything were to happen to you."

I hugged him tight and emotions bit at the backs of my eyes. I loved my father. Loved him so much. He had been my best friend and only confidante for so many years. I was so lucky to have him. "I will always be cautious," I told him. "But I need you to have faith in me. That I can do big, scary things. And that I can win."

He pressed a kiss to the top of my head and squeezed me a little tighter. "That isn't an easy ask, my dear. But I promise, I'll do my best, Margot."

We got better and better at battle magic over the next two days. And I kept dreaming of Olin. Conversations, him following me. In one, I was chasing after him through my house, and when I woke up, I was standing at the back door with my hand on the knob, in the very act of opening it to walk outside.

I'd sleepwalked as a child. Mom and Dad would find me in their bedroom or the bathroom. Once, I made it all the way outside to the sidewalk.

It had been at least seven years since I'd done it though.

We needed to find Olin, and put an end to this, so my mind could finally find some peace.

We worked even harder that day and Mary-Beth started getting on the phone, working with a booking agent to get our flights to England booked. The soonest we could all go would be in six days.

Six days, and then we would see if we were prepared.

I'd stayed up late that night, long after Nathaniel had fallen asleep. I didn't want to dream of Olin. I didn't want to go to bed only to wake up and do the same thing over in the morning. Instead, I found myself sitting with Mare McGregor's journal in my lap.

I still hadn't read it. It sat like a weight of guilt in the back of my brain every day. I'd made progress in taking it out the other day. It had set on my nightstand for a week now. It was always there, telling me I was a horrible human being because I wouldn't read it. My ancestor was killed for being a mage. I wanted to know the history of our kind. But I couldn't bring myself to sit and read this journal.

Not after what I'd seen in Salem.

It was too real. The danger. The reality that real people were killed for being able to do what I could do. She was my blood. My relative. And she had been murdered.

It made the danger and the reality that I could be killed too real.

That was all it took to finally get me to go to sleep that night. I set the book back on the nightstand, avoiding it for one more night. I turned out the light, and I curled up under the blanket.

My sleep that night was filled with nightmares. Hanging bodies and crooked trees. I saw burning houses and unearthly screams as mages were burned. I ran from mobs who chased me through the streets with pitchforks and news cameras.

As I turned a corner, I stopped dead in my tracks.

There, in the middle of a cobblestone street, there was a throne. And sitting upon it was Olin. He wore a crown on his head, but it was made of floating purple flames that danced and circled his head.

He sat forward, his eyes fixing on mine darkly. "How long will you make us run?" he asked, staring straight into my soul.

I couldn't speak. All of my defenses and rebuttals caught in my throat. All of my reasons for keeping us hidden and safe stopped at the back of my throat and stayed put.

Olin got up from his throne and turned past it, walking further down the alley. My feet moved forward automatically to follow. He slipped around the corner and I picked up my pace.

Like a shadow, he drifted further and further down the alley. Out of sight and back into it. That crown of purple flames grew dimmer, shifting from the brilliant violet to a burnt black.

"How do you justify the murders?" I asked, calling after him as he continued to slip out of my vision. "Is that how you deal with people who don't give you what you want? Just…end their lives?"

"How simple you see it," Olin said, his voice a slithering echo reverberating off the walls around me. "That it simply boils down to yes and no. Wrong, right, left or right. One opinion or another. My wife is dead, Margot. My family members were killed by *them*. This is about trying to even the scales, Margot. If they cannot see the errors of the past, we must force them to take another look. An eye for an eye."

His words sent chills flashing over my entire body. He believed he was justified. Flaunted himself.

"You're wrong," I said, the words sticking in my throat.

I watched as Olin slipped between two buildings and stepped out into an open space. He finally stopped walking and turned to meet my eyes.

I stepped out onto sand, and realized I was on the beach. But it wasn't some unfamiliar beach in an ancient part of England that would match the buildings we had been weaving through.

It was the beach in front of my house.

"There's so much we could accomplish together, Margot," Olin said, his voice low and calm. "And someday you will understand."

He raised his hand up and snapped his fingers.

It was absolutely disorienting. The feeling of falling, mixed with the slow confusion of waking from a deep, deep sleep. I blinked, shaking my head, and tried to make my eyes focus.

The dawn was just barely creeping into the horizon, out over the ocean.

I really was standing on the beach, dressed in my pajamas.

And Olin stood in front of me.

Behind him, a misty green circle glowed, and through it, I could see an ancient house in the middle of a grass field.

"One way or another, you will help me, Margot Bell," Olin said.

In an instant, he was standing right in front of me. His hand whipped out, grabbing my pajama top by the front. Before I could even scream or react, he yanked me forward, and we both fell through the portal.

"No!" the scream ripped from my lungs as I stumbled through what felt like nothing more than air, despite the glowing green ring. My heart hammered painfully, fight and flight filling every ounce of my blood as I landed on my side, my palms digging into the dirt.

It had been dawn one moment, and the next, it was brilliantly bright, high noon sun. We fell out into a grassy clearing in front of a house. Tall grass surrounded us, and just there, there was an ancient stone house with wood shakes for a roof.

I watched in horror as the portal closed.

CHAPTER EIGHTEEN

"You're being blind, Margot," Olin said as he climbed to his feet.

The second I got to mine, I started running.

He shot a hand out in my direction, and instantly, that familiar cold electrocuted through my blood. I was frozen in place.

"You will help me, Margot," Olin said. He turned me around in mid-air, making me face him. His eyes were cold, yet filled with conviction. "No one has ever held more knowledge of magic than you, save for the Keepers of the archive, and that's long lost." He took a step forward, holding my gaze the entire time.

I was completely frozen, and I felt as if I were slowly dying, all of my internal organs crystalizing. I tried to move my hands, to do the clap. I tried to summon words, so I could inflict the fear whisper. But I was simply frozen.

"You will teach me, Margot," Olin said, his words icy and cold. "And with the time, I will make you understand. You will see why this must happen."

He turned and walked toward the cottage, and I moved along with him, suspended and frozen. He opened the door and had to duck to walk inside. Gently, he guided me in and through the door, and closed it behind us without touching it.

It took my eyes several seconds to adjust to the sudden change in light. There were only two smaller windows in the building, and I could hardly see anything. But as they adjusted, I saw that the entire building was one open space.

There was an ancient looking fireplace in the center of one wall. A rudimentary kitchen was set up in one corner. A ratty couch was against another wall, and there was a double sized bed along the other wall. A well-worn rug was laid out in the middle of the floor.

It looked…old. But as if someone had attempted to bring it from the seventeenth century to the twentieth.

I wanted to ask him what this place was. But I still couldn't move anything.

"There isn't anyone around for eight kilometers," Olin said, letting me float in the middle of the room. "Don't bother screaming. And you could try to run, but I know the land, and I would find you."

My heart was hammering faster and faster. I needed to get unfrozen, I needed to immobilize him, do anything I could to stop this. The cold was creeping deeper and deeper inside of me. I could feel my cells crystalizing by the moment.

"I don't want to use it, but if you make me, I will." My heart jumped all the way into my throat as his eyes turned to the corner.

There was a metal box there, larger than a dog cage, but far, far smaller than a room. There was a door to it, just bigger than me.

Olin's affinity was metal.

"Do I have your cooperation, Margot?" he asked.

Instantly, I felt my mouth loosen and a breath escaped my lungs with it.

I took one deep breath, diving straight down into the deepest and darkest depths of my fears.

"Feel my fear," I said, and like a great wave, it all rushed out of me at once.

As soon as it hit Olin, the weight of it physical, his grip on me released and I fell to the floor as he let out his first terrified scream.

I crashed to the wooden floorboards and tried to leap to my feet to run. But I laid there, still, frozen. My fingers slowly clawed at the floor, but it as was as if I were moving in slow motion. I could barely straighten my legs.

Olin screamed again, the frantic tone in his voice escalating with each moment. I was barely able to turn my neck to look in his direction and see him skittering around on the floor as he clawed at himself, the air, the ground, tormented by all of my directed fear.

I pulled myself to my hands and knees, but I was slower than a sloth. My shoulders and knees screamed out in pain, my joints too frozen to function. Every movement was agony.

But I had to get out. No matter how my joints screamed, no matter how I felt as if I were going to shatter apart, I had to get out. Once I was out in the sunlight, surely I would thaw faster and I could get away.

Olin continued to scream and writhe in terror. I heard him back into the table against the wall. I didn't look back as I heard him smash into it over and over again. His screams continued to escalate.

The door was seven feet away, which in my current state, felt like seven miles. I stretched my hand forward, feeling as if fissures were going to break out along my arm. I slid my knee forward. I was pretty sure my shin was shattering.

Four feet. Three.

My heart hammered as I reached forward. If I could just get out…

Olin's breath came out in ragged, feral huffs. The banging stopped.

My heart dropped as I heard the sound of feet on the floor.

I felt a spark of cold grip me and then disappear. A

mumbled cry of fear leapt from my throat as I tried to scramble forward faster.

My hand crossed the threshold of the door, just as the cold gripped me throughout my entire body once more, and I was dragged backward, back into the house.

"That was a foul, clever trick," Olin said, still huffing and making sounds of fear. He lifted me into the air and turned me to face him once again. His entire body was overwhelmed with spasms, like he had the shivers and wanted to run at the same time. His eyes were shadowed, and his skin looked as if it had been pulled tight across his entire frame. "But you'll pay for that one."

He moved his extended hand and the door to that metal box slid open.

It was agonizing, because I was freezing with every passing second. But with everything I had left in me, I reached for the pearls around my neck and pulled them free.

I couldn't move properly. But I could still access telekinesis. Just as Olin used his mental grip on me to direct me into the box, I used my mind, and I flung my curved blade at him.

I was thrown into the box, landing hard against the floor. I saw my blade slice through his right arm, just as the door swung closed and sealed shut.

Olin let out a scream of fury and agony, stumbling back against the table again. Using everything I had in me, I kneeled against the wall of the box and pressed my face to the tiny window cut into the door.

Blood rushed down his arm, pulsing thick and heavy.

"You witch," he said the words as if they were a curse and not the truth. He gripped his opposite hand over the wound, trying to slow the flow.

"I could heal that for you," I said, pressing my hands against the metal walls. "All you have to do is let me out."

His wild eyes whipped to me and the look on his face was absolutely wild. Still feeling the effects of my fear, mingled with the adrenaline rush from his injury, his expression was wide and wild. "You've pulled enough surprises on me for one day. And thankfully I was an attentive student."

I watched as gold dust seemed to swirl around his hand, and I knew the wound was healing. Healing oneself with magic didn't work nearly as effectively as healing someone else, but it did work. Just more slowly.

I considered my options. I could continue to try to smash him with objects inside the house. But how would I ever get out of this box if I knocked him out or killed him? I could use the fear whisper on him again, but he'd overcome it so quickly last time. I could clap at him, but again, what if I knocked him out or killed him?

I had to get him to let me out of this box.

"You've never been particularly forthcoming with what you know how to do," I said. I had to get him talking. It's what he wanted to do. And that would be how I turned things around to get myself out of here. "But considering you said I know the most magic, I assume you think I know more than you do."

I could feel my body loosening up slowly, my joints less painful, more freely able to move. "We've come to this head, Olin. How about we share what we know?"

He looked back at me and released his arm. There was still a two-inch long gash running down it, though it was only half the size it had been. "You think you're so clever, Margot."

I shrugged, feigning confidence and calm. "It was worth a shot."

Olin covered his wound with his hand again and resumed trying to heal himself. He walked across the house toward my box, his eyes fixed on me with ferocity. "You're a confusion of a woman. In these breaths, you are haughty arrogance. In another, you want to hide in that mansion of yours, pretending you don't exist."

"Not this again," I said, impatience leaking into my voice. "As you once said, we keep dancing around the same thing, over and over. Just accept it, Olin. I'm never going to round into your way of thinking."

He glared at me with heated darkness, but there was too much going on in his head at the moment to make a solid argument. I saw him squeeze his arm tighter before he turned and stormed out of the house, slamming the door closed behind him.

I let out a huge breath and slumped back against the walls of the prison cell he'd put me in. I was pretending all this bravado, but internally, I was freaking out.

We were supposed to go after Olin together. Not just me against him. Borden might have been brave enough to go after him on his own once, but I wasn't this… warrior. I was a teacher, a discoverer, a historian.

But I would fake it if it kept me alive.

Mentally, I started calculating how long it would be until they all realized I was missing. Dawn was just starting to show on the horizon when I'd woken on the beach. That would mean Nathaniel would probably be waking up in the next twenty minutes or so. If he woke and didn't find me in the bed and didn't find me anywhere in the house, how long until he would start wondering where I'd gone? Would he assume I'd left to my parents' house? For a walk? Maybe I'd run to the grocery store.

He might look for me for a few hours before he got worried enough to try and track me.

We had the map now, he had endless items around the house that were mine and had my DNA. He could track me. But how long until he grew concerned enough to do so?

And once the map revealed where I was, how long would it take him to get to the airport, get on a flight, and then drive to wherever I actually was?

It might take an entire day for Nathaniel to get here. Maybe longer.

I brushed my fingers back into my hair, letting out a huge huff.

Olin had tried to kill me before, when I discovered who he really was and that he had lied. But would he have brought me here, just to kill me? What good did that do? No, he'd said I knew more magic than anyone but the Keepers.

That had to be what he wanted. My knowledge.

He wouldn't kill me, but he obviously didn't intend on keeping me comfortable.

I just had to coerce him into letting me out. And then I was going to have to strike when he thought he had the upper hand.

Twenty minutes passed, then thirty. I was very slowly beginning to loosen up. The ice in my veins warmed and the stiffness in my joints began to relent.

Not that it did me much good while I was stuck in this metal box. There were plenty of things I could do, magic wise, while being trapped in here. But It wouldn't get me freedom if I killed Olin and stayed welded inside.

Finally, the door opened a good forty minutes later, and Olin came walking back in. The gash in his arm was healed, but badly. He wore a dark, determined expression on his face, one that looked like he was resolved to do whatever it took.

He stalked to my box, his eyes fixed on mine. He laid

his hands on either side of the tiny window, and glared death at me.

"We found a necromancer," I blurted out, the very first interesting thing that came to my mind.

Olin's eyes widened and he straightened slightly.

I nodded, trying not to look too desperate and afraid. "He's known he had magic since he was a boy. He brought his dog back from the dead. And when he was a teenager, he accidentally killed his father with one touch."

I had his attention. It was written on every inch of his face.

"He's been teaching us necromancy," I lied. I sat with my back pressed against the metal walls of that box, hating that I was in this position. I'd do whatever it took to get out. "I can hardly even describe the guilt I feel every time I've killed an insect, but they're the best test subjects we have. I'm not very good at it yet. Borden of course has mastered it. Nathaniel is coming along well. But we're all learning. Death and resurrection. Did you know they were possible?"

"I did not," Olin breathed out. His confession was honest.

"We're also mastering invisibility," I lied again. We'd tried to replicate the magic that was attached to the book by touch. But the book was in German, and despite Nathaniel's growing skills, he couldn't make sense of the words within. We'd failed to do any other kind of invisibility. "It's actually easier than you'd think."

If I was going to lie, I might as well lie as much as I could.

It was his interest that I needed. And I'd hooked him.

"As I said, Margot," Olin said, and it was reverence in his tone. "I believe you know more magic now, save for the Keepers."

I picked up a small pebble from the ground of my metal prison. It wasn't difficult to find a sharp corner and cut myself enough to draw blood. I performed Alchemy as easy as I breathed now. It took me a matter of seconds to transform the pebble into solid gold.

"I've been selfish so far with alchemy," I said as my eyes rose up to meet his astonished ones. "I haven't taught it to any others. Borden and Nathaniel have attempted it but failed. We all think it is due to my affinity for earth. I do wonder. Yours is metal. Gold is technically a metal. I have a theory that you could probably do alchemy easier than I could."

The door to my prison suddenly ripped open with a horrible screech. The metal bent and folded outward. Instantly, I was gripped by the cold once more, and Olin dragged me out of the box. He also took hold of the gold I'd just created. Carefully, he pinched it between his thumb and index finger.

"Wealth has never once been my goal, Margot," he said as his eyes shifted back to me. I tried to clutch at my throat, because it felt as if crushing fingers were wrapping around it. But I gained no more oxygen. "But there have been countless times that I was severely limited because I did not have the finances. And once more, you prove how cowardly you've been, hoarding potential and letting it go to waste."

I tried to speak, but the words couldn't escape my windpipe that was being restricted by magic.

"How do you even sleep at night?" Olin asked, once more looking at the gold I'd created. "Does the guilt not eat you alive?"

Something outside caught my eye. From my angle, I couldn't see what it was clearly, but I could swear there was the flicker of green light.

Olin continued to ramble. More about avenging those who had died. More about living in the light of day. More nonsense that got so many of our ancestors killed.

Another flash of movement drew my eyes back to the window, but it was either a figment of my imagination, or I'd been too late to catch it.

But then I *knew* I saw *someone* dart across the field outside, faster than I could catch.

I looked back at Olin.

Another movement, immediately followed by another.

My chest surged with hope as the sky outside started darkening, a few drops of rain fell outside, and the crack of thunder immediately followed the brilliant blaze of light that lit up the sky.

Olin whipped around to look out the window. His

knuckles grew white as he gripped the window sill, and he sucked in a hard breath.

Electricity crackled through the air, and there was this weighted silence that followed the thunder, as if the entire world was holding its breath.

The roof of the house ripped off with a great crack of noise. The walls exploded outward, and the floor exploded into a million splinters.

Something new gripped me from the inside out. As Olin's hand whipped out toward me, it felt as if he were squeezing all of my insides. Rage burned in his eyes, and in them, I saw vengeance. He lifted his hand, and instantly, my body rose into the air, and there he left me, suspended twenty feet above the chaos that instantly exploded.

There, right in front of the ruined house, was a glowing, green portal.

They'd come for me. And they'd done it by using the one magic we had feared.

A spark of relief ripped through me when I realized my mother was not among the mages, or Mary-Beth.

Weapons flung out. Lightning struck the ground just a foot from Olin, and for a moment, every one of us was blind. Olin whipped around, ripping my metal box into a million shreds that he sent after every single one of my mages. Each of them dodged them, defending themselves in their own ways. But it was not without injury. I watched in horror as a shard gouged

Thomas in the leg, as another one caught Julie in the side.

John's hands whipped out and black smoke poured from them, giving them all cover as Olin searched for them.

With the cover of darkness, Nathaniel and Borden—whose eyes were glowing brilliant white—positioned themselves on either side of Olin, Aleem and Alexandra filling in the gaps.

"Now!" Nathaniel bellowed.

With a quick motion of their hands, each of them clapped at him. His body went ridged, frozen and suspended in place momentarily, considering he was surrounded. And then he collapsed to the ground. His head flew back, hitting the pavement, hard.

Nathaniel didn't hesitate. He leapt on Olin, and once more I saw that savage side of Nathaniel take over.

His hands went straight to Olin's throat. I watched as his fingers tightened around his windpipe, his fingers digging into his flesh. Olin grabbed at Nathaniel, his own fingers digging and clawing into Nathaniel.

Nathaniel pulled a hand back, letting his fist loose, connecting with Olin's jaw. I heard the snap, even through the mess of the storm.

"Let me end him, Nathaniel!" Borden bellowed. He stood there, with electricity crackling out from his hands. His entire frame was shaking and quivering with the electricity radiating through his body. The rain picked up in intensity. Another bolt of lighting struck the ground, just five yards from everyone. "Move!"

But Nathaniel didn't even get a chance to respond. Suddenly, Nathaniel ripped backwards as a shard of metal hit him in the arm, gouging open a wound, and another struck him in the face at the same time, striking across his cheek before skittering off.

It gave him just enough of a window. Olin extended a hand, blasting Nathaniel off of him. He rolled and climbed to his feet, sending out a blast of icy air that sent everyone flying back fifteen feet.

"Now!" Dorian roared.

"Feel my fear!" came the cry and curse from Marie, Julie, Poppy, Alexandra and Thomas.

A manic scream ripped from Olin's throat when he heard the words. But nothing could stop what was coming for him.

It all struck him with the force of the devil, in the exact moment a bolt of lightning struck his body.

It was as if it happened in slow motion. The streak of blinding light hit his body, causing it to distort. His back arched. His eyes grew wide. His limbs splayed out, taut and out of control.

And in just a flash, the lightning was gone.

There was a web of blood red streaks over his entire body. Climbing up his face, down his arms. He was a walking nightmare.

Olin clawed at himself, even as horrified screams

ripped from his throat. His fingers left deep claw marks in his skin. He collapsed on himself, letting out sounds and shrieks that didn't sound earthly.

Nathaniel stalked forward through the torrential rain and grabbed Olin by the front of his shirt, hauling him to his feet.

"This is the fear you caused," he said, and the sound and power of Nathaniel's voice sent shivers down my spine. "You sparked the hunt of your own kind. You put so many in danger. For what? To be seen as someone better?"

Nathaniel shook his head, and in his eyes, I saw pity and disgust. Even as Olin continued to bellow in terror.

Nathaniel released him and Olin collapsed on the ground. He yelled and cried, his sounds coming out hoarse and ragged.

Magic glitched in the air. Some rain began to rise up instead of falling. A portal sparked behind Olin, but it flashed brilliant for just a second before going out. Cold washed through the air, turning some of the rain into snow.

But as Olin writhed in fear and pain, he couldn't get control of enough magic to help him.

My stomach dropped in horror. All of the metal shards that Olin wielded had been frantically flying through the air during his fear assault. But suddenly, they stopped. They all paused. They turned in the air.

They all hesitated there, quivering and poised. The air seemed to hum with them, just waiting…waiting.

"It is all in vain," he said. His words came out rough, desperate. But filled with pain and disappointment. "Everything you have done, and you choose to hide it away." He shook his head. "Do not let it all have been for nothing."

And then every single shard of metal launched at Olin.

I cringed, looking away just a second too late, as every piece of metal in the air embedded itself into Olin's body.

Blood oozed from him instantly. Great rivers erupted from nearly every square inch of his flesh, and within seconds, he was covered in red.

Olin sucked in a hiss of a breath as he was pierced.

One beat. I watched the frantic gleam in his eyes grow a little duller.

Two. It leached out of his body, right along with his blood.

I heard the air exhale from his wheezy, punctured lungs.

And then I was falling through the air.

The house had been destroyed. But the ruins of it lay beneath me.

It all happened so fast and slow at the same time. I twisted as I fell. I saw the wall beneath me, ruins of rubble and stone. I twisted further, and there was the stormy sky.

Pain seared through my back. There was a chain of crunching sounds. Sharp agony ripped through every nerve in my body. White hot pain blinded me. And then I heard another crack, all too loud in my skull. I felt a bounce. My entire body was filled with blinding white pain.

And then…there was nothing.

CHAPTER NINETEEN

Death was less peaceful than I expected.

I could tell I was no longer tethered to a body. Because I could see myself, lying there on that rock wall, broken and still. I could see the chaos that surrounded me, as everyone stared at Olin, dead and lifeless as well.

I could feel the horror. I couldn't tell if it was my own. Or if it was simply flooding the air, emitted from everyone around me.

But I could feel myself dissolving. Growing thinner, less…here, with every passing second.

One second, everyone was staring at Olin, waiting for him to scream, to move, to breathe.

Two seconds, Nathaniel glanced over his shoulder.

Three seconds, he registered what he was seeing.

Chaos and fear and urgency. They all burned through the air with intensity.

I could see it as Nathaniel reached me and paused, for just a second, unsure if he should move me or not.

"Margot," he breathed out. He gripped my shoulders, hesitating for just another second. "Margot!"

They didn't get a moment to take in the fact that Olin was dead. They didn't get to celebrate a victory. They didn't have time to process that in the end, they didn't actually have to kill Olin. He'd done it himself to end the madness and fear they'd inflicted upon him.

Everyone darted to my side.

"Margot!" Borden bellowed. His eyes flashed infinitely brighter, and all at once, the sky split apart. Eight lightning bolts hit the ground, a perfect circle around everyone. Their hair stood on end. Their bodies shook with the intensity of the thunder that instantly ripped through the air. All of the oxygen was sucked from the circle.

But Borden was at my side in an instant and pulled my body from Nathaniel's grip, dragging me down to the ground and off the wall. Nathaniel yelled something about causing further injury.

Poppy let out a horrified whisper. "Why isn't she moving?"

"She's unconscious," Thomas stated matter of factly.

I could feel myself dissolving further, getting thinner and thinner.

Nathaniel knelt beside me, gently shaking me, saying my name. "Margot," he said, but the tone of his whisper told me he had an inkling of the truth. "Margot, wake up."

But Borden pulled his hand away from my head, and it was coated entirely in my blood. Nathaniel froze when he saw it, and every ounce of color leached from his face.

Borden placed his fingers to the side of my neck, and every single one of them was still and silent.

I watched Borden go white and then a sick shade of green.

"She's dead?" Abigale asked with a hoarse whisper.

"No," John said, shaking his head and backing up three steps. "No, no, no."

Poppy's eyes filled with tears and a rough sob ripped from her lips. Alexandra wrapped her arms around her stomach as if she were going to be sick. Marie and Julie hugged each other, staring at my body lying limply there.

Nathaniel looked at me, looking empty and devoid of life. He was so still. It was unnatural, as if he'd been turned to stone and emptied of a soul.

But I saw it, the moment something struck Borden. His shoulders stiffened and he sat up straighter. His head whipped up, searching the faces that surrounded him. "Aleem!"

The young man startled hard at the harsh, powerful way Borden spoke his name.

I didn't have a stomach any longer. Or a heart. But all of those things felt as if they reacted at the realization.

"Bring her back," Borden said. And the intense way

his glowing eyes were fixed upon Aleem, the way he spoke his words, there was a promise behind his words. If he failed, Borden's reaction would not be anything anyone wanted to witness.

These past few weeks, we'd had a necromancer at our school.

Necromancers cannot be trained. They were born. Within certain lines, certain witches were born with the ability to raise the dead.

"I…" Aleem stuttered. "I don't know how…"

Finally, Nathaniel moved. Hope surged in his eyes. He sucked in a sharp breath and his eyes flickered to Aleem. He laid a hand on his shoulder. There was so much tenderness and brokenness in his expression, it fractured my soul a little farther. "Please, Aleem. You must try. She…" Emotion cracked his ability to speak. He swallowed and looked back down at my body, at my bleeding head, at the *wrong* way I was lying. "She is *everything*. You must try."

Aleem shook his head. "I might bring her back. But she will still be broken."

"We can heal her," Nathaniel said, the determination settling into his expression. "All of us." He looked around, and every single one of the mages nodded in agreement.

They all stepped up. Marie. Julie. Poppy. Peter and Thomas. John, Dorian, Abigale, and Alexandra. Nathaniel laid his hands on either side of my head.

Borden placed his hands on my chest, right over my heart.

By the moment, I felt myself dissolving more. I felt the pull to…somewhere else. With every second that passed, I felt like I couldn't stay.

The air below me glowed. Gold dust swirled around, gathering from each of my mages. My broken body grew lighter and lighter, glowing brilliant and golden.

Aleem looked absolutely terrified. So much had gone awry when he'd tried his necromancy. He'd done it on accident. He'd risen horrors and accidentally killed his own father.

We couldn't train him how to use his abilities. He was alone in that.

And now they were asking him to harness the ability and raise his own teacher from the dead.

His hands were shaking intensely as he removed his gloves. He was pale as could be as his eyes slid down to me.

He came to stand above me, and I could read his terror in every surface of his face.

But I was so, so proud of him as he reached his hand down.

I felt lighter. I felt less like a soul…like a person…and more like air.

Time was fading.

Aleem reached down, and finally his hand came into contact with my cheek.

The world erupted into demonic howls and flashes of red…black…white. Blinding and wicked, my existence flashed in whips of motion and sound. The entire world rumbled with this…bellow. My vision faded to black and my entire being vibrated intensely. I had the sensation of being sucked through a tube and rocketing forward with terrifying speed.

I threw out a hand to stop myself, and felt it come into contact with someone's chest. I tried to suck in a breath, but there was still blood in my lungs, even though there was less and less with every passing second.

My back screamed in agony, and one second I couldn't feel my toes, and then the next, I could. Sensations of utter excruciating pain ripped up my legs, through my thighs, into my back.

My back arched up off the ground as I tried to escape the pain.

I felt like my body was filled with a million fire ants trying to escape and hide. My body was unsure how to reaccept my soul as Aleem re-directed it back inside. It fought back for the peace and silence it had gained for a few short minutes.

Finally, the blood cleared from my lungs, and I sucked in a terrified gasp.

I could feel dozens of hands on me. I could feel magic coursing through my veins, flooding from them into me. Fiber by fiber, bone by bone, muscle by muscle, my family healed my broken body, knitting me back together into a whole person.

Dark, so dark, I was lost in the depths of this reunification. I gasped in another breath, trying to suck in more oxygen, because it felt real and human.

Slowly, the ants in my blood dissolved. They died and obliterated themselves into my bloodstream, being washed away by the tide.

Slowly, the agony in my entire body ceased.

Slowly, I felt the river flooding from my head cease.

Slowly, I felt my heart catching up.

And finally, I opened my eyes.

CHAPTER TWENTY

The sounds of sleep surrounded me. Soft snores and deep, long pulls of breath. They were here in this room, on the floor, and in the next. I sat with my back against the headboard, looking around at them all.

After I had awoken from death, my mages tried to rush me to the hospital, which had not been an easy task, considering we were out in the middle of nowhere. Thankfully, a farmer had seen us walking and had let all of us pile into his truck as he gave us a ride.

But at least I was thinking clearly. I could feel my body. I felt no pain. Nothing felt broken. Considering I had just broken my back and fractured my skull, I felt incredible.

I knew they all had healed me. I had faith in their abilities.

But my fractures and breaks might still show on

hospital scans. The doctors might ask questions, and we wouldn't be able to answer them with logical explanations they would accept.

"I'm not going to the hospital," I'd insisted as we bumped along in the back of the truck.

"You just died," Nathaniel said, looking at me pointedly. "You need medical attention."

"I'm fine!" I insisted. "There's nothing they can do for me."

Though he didn't say anything, I could feel the anger and frustration rolling off of Borden. The clouds once more thickened and darkened about a mile out.

"Fine," Nathaniel said through gritted teeth.

"Why do you just give in to her?" Borden finally shouted. "You know as well as I do that she needs to be seen. And you're just giving up?"

"Borden!" It wasn't just me that yelled at him. But Marie, Julie, Alexandra, and Poppy, all at once.

He'd fallen silent, but still fumed.

I didn't go into the hospital, and I didn't give anyone else the chance to argue with me. Nathaniel simply took my hand and pressed a kiss to the back of it.

We had all agreed that it wasn't worth the risk of trying the portal magic again. We needed to get home. But now that there was no urgency, why risk going through once more, only for something to go wrong?

So here we were tonight, crammed into the only two hotel rooms available, waiting for morning when we would fly home on a privately chartered plane. Considering we wanted to go home immediately, and how many of us there were, it was our cheapest option.

It was probably pushing one in the morning. Considering the time difference from here in England to home, I was a little surprised that everyone was actually asleep. I found myself the sole survivor in the fight against the night.

I was so grateful for all of them. Every single one of them. They knew there was a chance that they might get hurt, or even die. They knew what had happened to my mother, and still, every single one of them charged through the portal to come save me.

They'd dedicated their lives to learning magic. To furthering our kind. They'd become a part of this family, this community. They'd fought for each other and our race.

Nathaniel rolled over, slinging an arm around my waist. In the dark, his eyes fluttered open and he met my own. "Can't sleep?" he whispered.

I shrugged. "Just…thinking too much."

He shifted closer, touching his forehead to my cheek. "I have a feeling you spend more than a few nights like this."

I gave a little smile, because he was right, and he understood that about me so well. "You know, just contemplating life and death and all of that, considering I got to visit it today."

Nathaniel grew still and heavy at that. He tightened his grip on me a little bit. "I could see where people lose their minds. When you were lying there…my mind could not accept it. I couldn't even contemplate that what was happening in front of me was real."

Through the dark, my eyes searched for the door that opened into the other room. There, on the floor, Aleem slept, his peaceful face toward me. "Maybe it's because you knew we had the means to bring me back."

Nathaniel shook his head. "I think it's because I truly cannot imagine a world without you in it, Margot. Those months when we weren't together… They were the worst times of my life. I hope you realize what you're getting yourself into. Because I need you like I need oxygen. And you're never going to get rid of me."

I rolled over, placing my hand against his cheek. The light was dim, barely peeking around the curtains. But I could make out his eyes in the dark. Green and intense, and absolutely honest in this moment. "I think you underestimate just how in love with you I am. From the moment I met you in that library at Alderidge, over a strange book that I could only read when I touched it, I was gone. Done for. It was always meant to be you and me, Nathaniel. For good."

The intensity smoldered in Nathaniel's eyes. He leaned forward, and his lips met mine. They were so tender yet confident. They spoke a million promises and reciprocated my words.

We were always meant for each other. From the very beginning.

THE FLIGHT WAS WONDERFUL. Borden and Mary-Beth might have experience chartering private jets for international travel, but it was certainly a first for the rest of us. The pilot asked no questions. There was no mess over the fact that not a single one of us had our passports. We could simply sit back and enjoy the plush seats and the relaxation of something that felt so human.

We touched down at a smaller airport, and there waiting for us, were my tearful and anxious parents.

Mom wrapped me in her arms and immediately started sobbing. Dad grabbed me and held me so tight I could hardly breathe.

I was so grateful that the events of that day happened at a time when Mom wasn't there. It was early in the morning. It was kind of a miracle that John and Dorian were there at the house, considering they didn't live there. But Mom hadn't yet arrived for the lessons that day, so she never came through the portal to fight Olin.

I was thankful for that.

"I can't believe…any of it," Mom said through her tears. "You… and Olin… and everything."

She continued sobbing.

"It's okay, Mom," I said, running my hand down her

hair. "I'm perfectly healthy. They all did great. You would have been so proud of them all."

I leaned back, smiled at her, and wiped her tears away.

We all loaded up into the two cars, absolutely crammed to the maximum. We made the twenty-minute drive back to the house, and everyone sighed in relief when we walked through the doors. Khan barked in happy relief, running right up to Nathaniel and licking him everywhere. He already came up to Nathaniel's hips.

And there was Mary-Beth, standing in the entryway.

She was crying before I even walked in. She looked so angry, and emotionally destroyed. I just walked up to her, wrapped my arms around her, and together, we sobbed for a good two minutes.

And then she ranted. About everything. About the injustice of being locked and missing out and being the fragile, useless one. And how we were all reckless in everything we did. On and on, Mary-Beth went. She just needed to let it out. It was her way of coping. And we all let her, because…we were trying to understand. She was the only locked among us.

And then everything was okay.

We picked up dinner, and everyone was happy and chatty and full of life as we ate together.

We'd done it. Overcome someone who wanted to expose our kind…someone who had created such chaos and strife.

We could do this. No matter what came our way, we could overcome it. Our ancestors had been killed and hunted in the past. But we had learned from their history. We had been more prepared. We knew the dangers. And we would meet them head on.

By the end of the day, things felt…normal. I hugged Dorian and John when they had to leave for the day. I'd thanked them profusely before they left, and they'd done so with a kiss to my forehead and a promise to return on Monday when we would resume classes.

Marie and Julie drifted up to their bedroom. Abigale and Alexandra settled into a game of chess. Thomas wandered off to find Mary-Beth, who was still stewing just a little bit in her room. Aleem retired to his room.

He was looking at me with absolute terror now. He'd done it, and everyone had sung his praises. But his fear was what might happen if he ever touched me again? Would I die again?

We didn't know, and so it could never, ever happen.

But as Nathaniel took Khan for a quick walk, I wandered out onto the back deck and sank into a chair. Just a few moments later, Borden stepped outside as well.

I offered him a small smile and watched as he settled into the chair beside me.

Together, we sat there for a solid three minutes, not saying a word, simply looking out over the ocean as the sun set somewhere behind us.

Sometimes it was so easy with Borden.

It was hard to imagine that once upon a time, he ran around with the Society Boys. That he'd physically harmed Nathaniel, that he'd helped David Sinclair corner me and annoy me endlessly. Once upon a time, I didn't trust him at all when he'd shown up at Nathaniel's solarium and showed us the magic he could do.

So many things had changed.

"I think you and Nathaniel should move up the wedding," he said, and they were the last words in the world I would have expected him to say.

I looked over at him, a deep V furrowing between my brows.

He didn't look at me, just continued to stare out over the ocean. "What you and Nathaniel have, you're exceptionally lucky. It's something rare and special. The two of you…" Borden shook his head and his fingers curled around the arm of the chair. "When you died, the look on Nathaniel's face…" He paused again, and I was lost in the complexity of the emotions on Borden's own face. "I love you, Margot. And I'm not sure what it is going to take to change the way I feel. But what *I* feel… It is not the same as what Nathaniel feels for you. He's… good, and pure, and he is going to love you the way you should be loved for the rest of your life."

This was hard for Borden to say, I could see it in every inch of his tight shoulders and his anxious hands. But I could also see…relief, coming off of him in flakes. As if he were shedding the weight.

"So, I don't know why in the world you would wait a moment longer to marry that man, Margot," Borden said, and finally, he turned to look at me. And in his eyes, I could see just how much he meant every single word he said.

They tightened my throat and sent electricity through all my blood. This right here, this was why I did love Borden. Because we could be honest and raw with each other. We could tell each other the truth, even when it might break our own hearts.

"Thank you, Borden," I said in a hoarse whisper.

CHAPTER TWENTY-ONE

I T WAS STRANGE TO REALIZE JUST HOW ACCUSTOMED to sleeping beside Nathaniel I really had become. The night before the wedding, we had gone with tradition. Nathaniel had slept upstairs with the boys in a massive sleepover. The girls and I had spent the night in my room, having our own bachelorette party, playing games, doing gifts, and generally having one of the best nights of my life.

But the fact that I didn't sleep very much that night had very little to do with the late night, the extra sounds of sleep, or the fact that the biggest day of my life was coming the next night.

It was the fact that I missed Nathaniel beside me.

But morning finally dawned, and I mentally told myself that I would not be tired. No matter what. Not today.

Poppy went into the kitchen and made a gigantic breakfast. I got into the shower while it was cooking and was immediately accosted by Mary-Beth and Marie the second I was in a towel. They combed through my hair and set it into gigantic rollers. They oiled my skin up with three different kinds of creams and lotions, assuring me that I was going to be radiant. Finally, I was allowed to slip on a robe and step out into the rest of the house to go eat.

The house was already bustling with life. Mom was in full directorial mode, telling my father and Thomas and Peter where to move things. Everyone else was moving around the kitchen, grabbing things to eat, and then spreading throughout the house or outside to eat.

I spotted Nathaniel with his back turned to me, grabbing something from the counter. I slid up behind him and wrapped my arms around his waist.

He turned and looked down at me with a charming smile on his face.

"Well good morning, Miss Bell," he said as he slipped his hands down to my hips, covered only by my thin, silky bathrobe.

"Come tomorrow morning, you can no longer call me that," I cooed to him.

He made a low growling sound in the base of his throat. I remembered his request. For me not to mention the name Margot Nightingale again until we were married. "Did I tell you that you look stunning?"

If it were any other person, I would think they were making fun of me, considering what I was wearing, the fact that my hair was in these curlers, and that I wasn't wearing an ounce of makeup. But coming from Nathaniel, I knew it was genuine, and that he truly meant every word. "No, maybe you should tell me more about it."

"Save it for tonight, you two," Mary-Beth said teasingly as she pushed me away from Nathaniel. "All this ridiculous sexual tension after two years of holding out. You're going to make the entire house explode if you get any closer."

I laughed, eyeing Nathaniel hungrily as she pushed me toward the table.

"Sit, stay," she commanded. "I'm making you a plate and you have to eat."

Nathaniel looked at me and it wasn't hard to imagine all the things he was thinking of doing to me. But Thomas bumped him with his shoulder, knocking him off his trail of thought, and grabbed something to eat.

The beginning of the day was beautiful chaos. The reception was planned to be both indoors and out. We had to set up tables and chairs. We decorated the tables. The caterers showed up just after two o'clock and started setting up and cooking. We had to set up the arch down at the beach and drape the tule and flowers for the walkway.

I tried to help. I really did. I wasn't one to let others

do the hard work and just sit on the sidelines. But others kept telling me to go away. To relax and enjoy my big day.

So, while everyone finished setting up down at the beach, I found myself floating through the house. I wandered up to my office and stared out over the ocean.

We'd worked so hard. The past two years had been fraught with so much work and uncertainty. I'd died just two weeks ago.

But I would do it all over again. Go through all of that struggle just to be here.

I looked down at the journal in my hand. I'd been meaning to read Mare McGregor's journal for so long now, ever since we'd found it in Salem. It had sat like a weight in the back of my mind, causing me oceans of guilt.

But I'd come to realize that I didn't need this part of the past. We'd collected enough. We had learned enough lessons. I didn't need to feel the pain of what happened to my ancestor any deeper than I already did. After having a vision of her hanging in Salem, I was scarred. I could let this one small bit of the past go and close this door.

I walked to the bookshelves along the back wall. I filed Mare's journal with a row of others, and instantly, I felt relief. The guilt lifted off my shoulders.

It was time to focus on the future. Because I was exactly where I wanted to be, now.

I couldn't imagine being happier.

Especially so when Nathaniel wandered up the stairs.

My eyes met his, just for a moment. In them, every moment of heat and passion was there. His green eyes said everything. A new scar stood out on his cheek, still angry and red from our fight with Olin. But it didn't mar his beauty one bit.

He wore a pair of black slacks and a white button up shirt that wasn't buttoned. I couldn't help myself when my eyes cut straight to his chiseled torso. They traced up his abdominal muscles, up between the valley between his chest. Up this throat. And finally, my eyes met his.

"You're trying to destroy my sense of tradition in the last two hours before the knot is tied?" I asked as I stepped forward. My hands didn't hesitate, they cut through his shirt and came to his chest, skin to skin.

"I am a man of principle, Margot," he said, but still, he ran his hand up my arm to clasp his hand around my wrist, keeping it firmly planted against his bare skin. "I would never try to corrupt you."

"Says the man who snuck into my bedroom and pushed me down onto my bed for our very first kiss," I teased him.

He smiled at the memory, but he didn't say anything. His free hand just slid to the back of my neck and he pulled me forward. A soft sound escaped my throat when his lips met mine, and I didn't hesitate in letting him into my mouth. His tongue stroked and danced with mine.

My hands slid down to his sides, pulling Nathaniel greedily to me.

Who cared about a couple of hours? We'd waited long enough.

"Are you kidding me?" Mary-Beth's voice cut sharply through the air. I yanked back from Nathaniel as she stomped up the spiral stairs. She cut straight to me, grabbed me by the wrist, and started dragging me back to the stairs. "I leave you alone for two minutes, and you two are sneaking off to dry hump when it's really time to get dressed. You'll have the go ahead in 120 minutes. You've waited this long."

"But, I-" I tried to protest as I looked back at Nathaniel, who was blushing fiercely and buttoning up his shirt.

"No buts!" Mary-Beth called as she dragged me down the stairs.

I blushed even harder when I got to the bottom and found all of my favorite women in the world waiting to help get me ready.

"You ready?" Mom asked.

And it really hit me.

I was about to get married. Bound for the rest of my life.

"Let's do this," I said.

They pulled and pinned my hair. They dabbed and brushed. Every one of them worked me over from head to toe. Hair, makeup, nails, skin. I felt like a doll as they worked every single surface of my body. I had no privacy as I changed into the appropriate underthings to go under my dress.

My heart leapt into my throat when I heard the doorbell, over and over. Guests were arriving and Thomas and Peter acted as ushers, taking people to their places down on the beach.

Soft music started playing and floated all the way in here to the master bathroom.

I started getting nervous and anxious.

Only a few more minutes.

"The moment we've all been waiting for," Mom said as she retrieved the white garment bag from the closet. She was glowing. I wasn't sure I'd ever seen her so happy as she unzipped it and pulled my dress from it.

I wasn't sure I'd ever felt happier either.

I ran my hands over the lace and silk, completely enthralled with the dress.

"Come on ladies," I said. "Help me get into my wedding dress."

They each squealed and stepped up to the task with excitement.

It fit like a glove, and as I turned and looked in the mirror, I was reminded why this dress felt like magic.

It hugged me in every right way. It made me feel like a princess in my own fairy tale. I could do anything in this dress, conquer any obstacle that stood in the way of me and Nathaniel, in this dress.

And then Mary-Beth stepped up behind me and carefully placed the veil into my hair.

"You look beautiful, Margot," Mom said as she placed her hands on my shoulders. She radiated with her smile. Her eyes were misty, but the tears didn't fall and ruin her own perfect makeup.

I reached up a hand and placed it over hers, and marveled that I got this opportunity, to have my mother with me on the day of my wedding.

"I think it's time," Poppy said, beaming at me.

I turned around, facing them all. Every one of them looked so lovely in their pale pink dresses. They beamed at me, and I was just so happy that they looked so happy. "Thank you," I said, my chest swelling with emotion. "All of you. It's been the perfect day, and that's in part because of every single one of you."

There were six of them there. The most important women in my life. My mother. Mary-Beth. Poppy, Julie, and Marie. Abigale and Alexandra. My family. My students. My best friends.

"Let's get you married, huh?" Mary-Beth said, ever herself.

I beamed as we all bustled around. Mom handed me my bouquet, and then they all shuffled out of the room to take their places and tell everyone that we were ready to get started.

As the last of them slipped out the door, a new face appeared. My father blushed as he stepped inside, dressed in his suit. Instantly, his eyes welled, and he pressed a fist to his mouth.

"Dad," I said, fighting my own emotion as I saw his overwhelm him. I crossed the bedroom to him and pulled him into a hug.

He sucked in a deep breath and wrapped his arms around me, clinging to me tight. "I'm just so incredibly proud, Margot," he said. "You've created so much. You've been so brave. You've built this incredible life. And now you're moving onto the next step."

"I'll always be your little girl," I promised him. "It will always be you and me as a team."

Dad nodded and backed away to look into my eyes. "I know," he said. "And I couldn't possibly imagine a better team member to join. I couldn't have asked for a better son-in-law than Nathaniel. He's perfect for you."

I nodded, because it was entirely true.

The door cracked open, and Mary-Beth's face appeared. "Ready?" she asked.

Dad quickly wiped away his tears and put on his smile. I straightened, adjusting my grip on my bouquet. I looped my arm through Dad's, and then nodded to her. "Ready."

She opened the door wide, and I watched as the procession of the bridal party walked through the living room and then out onto the deck.

And when it came to our turn, I stepped forward with my father, and my heart skyrocketed in my chest.

We made our way through the living room, then stepped out into the brilliant sunshine outside on the deck. My eyes immediately searched for Nathaniel down on the beach, but my view of him was blocked by the sea grasses. So, with patience, because it was proper, I didn't run. I walked in the procession, in time with the music. Down the stairs. Across the grass. And then we turned down the stone path that dropped down to the beach.

And there he was.

Standing there beneath the arch, dressed in a pale gray suit, stood the love of my life.

The smile that spread on Nathaniel's face the moment we saw each other surely could have powered Nightingale Academy for an entire year. He didn't hide it one little bit when his eyes slid from my face, down my bust, down to the end of my dress, and then back up. I blushed, because I could see in his eyes all the things he was thinking about doing. And mixed just as equally with his heat, was his love.

In his eyes, I could see our entire future. I could hear his promises. His oath to love me and fight for us for the rest of his days.

He looked happier and more brilliant than any moment in his entire life.

I couldn't help it. My face broke into a smile as well, and my entire chest swelled with love and happiness.

He looked so amazing. His suit hugged his tall frame. His hair was tamed and exact. He looked like a Norse god, standing there, waiting for me on the beach.

I was about to marry that man.

Suddenly I walked a little faster, and Dad just chuckled, patting my hand.

I didn't even notice that everyone in the audience was standing until I was nearly past them all. But they didn't stand a chance at holding my attention. Not when Nathaniel stood there at the finish line.

Finally, finally, finally, I reached him. Our eyes were locked on one another as I stepped in front of him. My father pressed a kiss to my cheek as he placed my hand in Nathaniel's.

And an overwhelming feeling of peace settled into me as we touched.

This was exactly where we were supposed to be. Here, together, saying vows.

"Margot," Nathaniel whispered as he looked me up and down, his eyes filled with absolute wonder. "You look…" He was at a loss for words.

"I think you should just wear this suit, for the rest of forever," I said, not hiding it as I looked him over once more. "You know, during the daylight hours."

The pastor cleared his throat, and I blushed to remember that we were not alone.

Everyone in the wedding party standing to our sides

and sitting in the front row laughed, not a one of them surprised.

The pastor started talking then, but the words meant very little to me in that moment. I knew what this meant, standing here with Nathaniel, before all of our friends and family. He was a prop, a necessity. I'd already made the commitment. He just made it official.

"Repeat after me," he said, finally.

"Margot, I promise to love you," Nathaniel began, his eyes locked on mine. "In good times and in bad, when life is easy, but especially when it is hard. I promise to love you when our love is simple, and when it is an effort. I promise to cherish you, and to always honor you. These things I give to you today, and all the days of our life."

My heart fluttered in my chest. It was everything I could do to not rush forward and kiss him right then.

He lifted my left hand and slid on a simple gold band to join the other ring on that finger.

I beamed with love and excitement.

"Margot, repeat after me," the pastor said.

"Nathaniel, I promise to love you." Time seemed to slow, and I felt every single word coming from my mouth, from the tips of my toes, to the end of every single hair on my head. "In good times and in bad, when life is easy, but especially when it is hard. I promise to love you when our love is simple, and when it is an effort. I promise to cherish you, and to always honor you. These things I give to you today, and all the days of our life."

Mary-Beth handed me the simple gold ring. I had gone into Nathaniel's solarium and found a pebble that had been left inside. I'd turned it to gold, and brought it to the jeweler to be custom made. With a blush, I turned back to Nathaniel and took his hand. With a smile that was making my cheeks ache, I slipped it onto his finger.

"Ladies and gentlemen, I present to you, Mr. and Mrs. Nightingale," the pastor said with a smile. "You may kiss your bride."

Finally. I rushed forward at the same time Nathaniel's hand locked behind my neck, crushing his lips to mine. I melted into that kiss, his lips moving with mine in utter desperation. We inhaled, breathing each other's air and needing nothing more.

I had fought for this man since the day we'd met. I'd known he was meant to be mine for so long now. We'd grown together and fought together. We'd overcome differences and come to appreciate our similarities.

We had forever now.

Nathaniel and me. The two of us. For the rest of our lives.

The cheering of the crowd reminded me that we were not alone. Regretfully, I removed my lips from Nathaniel's, staring into his eyes for a moment.

I saw excitement there. I saw promises, that he would always make me happy and sometimes he would challenge me, but it would always be worth it.

I couldn't wait.

Nathaniel took my hand and turned toward the audience, raising them together in the air triumphantly.

The crowd called and cheered and generally celebrated the very best day of my life.

I looked over at my husband, and my entire being filled with so much happiness. He yanked me back to him, wrapping his arms around me, and dipped me low in a soul melding kiss.

THE RECEPTION WAS BOTH BEAUTIFUL, and excruciatingly long. We had immediately gone from the wedding to the dinner inside. The room was buzzing and loud with talks and cheers and the sounds of dinner being eaten.

I looked up more than once, grinning from ear to ear at seeing Laurel, Nathaniel's sister, sitting with my mom and dad, talking happily, with her husband Raymond at her side. It was only fair that we both had family here. They chatted, only too thrilled to get to know Nathaniel's biological family after believing that they would never get the opportunity to do so.

When dinner was over with, we headed back outside, into the darkening night. The deck was massive enough that we all fit without an issue. Music started, and I knew it was time.

Nathaniel extended a hand toward me. With a smile, I accepted it, and he pulled me into his arms.

Slowly, we began to sway back and forth to the music. I was in absolute wonder as I looked up at Nathaniel.

"Did you know that President John Adams met his wife, Abigail when she was only fifteen?" he asked. And I could only smile and shake my head, because I would have expected nothing less from him. Nathaniel smiled, and my heart skipped a beat. "He was twenty-four, so there was quite the age gap. But they courted years later and married when she, too, was twenty years old."

"You don't say," I said. Really, in this moment, I didn't necessarily care about the history. But coming from Nathaniel, it was romantic, and I held on to his every word.

He nodded. "The newlyweds rode off on a single horse together. Over the years, they had five children. And together, they witnessed revolution, war, scandal, diplomatic crises. They were often separated due to his career. Over a forty-year course, they wrote over one thousand letters to each other, most of them descriptive love letters."

"That's very sweet," I said, looking up into the eyes of my new husband.

"Abigail wasn't just his wife, the mother of his children," Nathaniel said, gazing down at me. "She was his advisor in politics and life. She was a diplomat and an exceptionally progressive first lady. And through their fifty years of marriage, they never grew tired of each other."

Nathaniel leaned forward and pressed his forehead to mine. "You are my partner, Margot. My equal or better in every single way. And I never will understand how I got so fortunate in life."

As I looked into his eyes, I could hardly believe the man Nathaniel had turned out to be. Patient and kind, smart and wonderful. He'd overcome so much and grown into this person I respected more than anyone in the entire world.

"I think I'm the lucky one," I breathed out. I reached a hand up, cupping it behind his head. Nathaniel knew exactly what I wanted. He pressed his lips to mine, and every cell in my body zinged with life, driving me desperate. I pressed myself closer, deepening the kiss, and Nathaniel happily obliged. His hands slipped from my waist, down over my rear end, pulling our bodies closer together.

Out in the crowd, there were sighs of envy, a few cat calls of encouragement, and I could just *hear* the eye roll from Mary-Beth.

I smiled, backing up from Nathaniel. The song changed, and I extended a hand for my girls, pulling them in to dance with me to the fast-paced beat.

It was so fun. Dancing and being crazy. And then slowing down and having dances with my parents. We all swapped partners and talked and laughed.

And when it came time for Borden's turn, we just danced slow, having another one of our silent conversations.

He was happy for me. I knew that he was. This was what I wanted. This was what he knew was best.

But it was still hard.

He'd kissed my cheek when it was over, and then John and Dorian came to steal me for a dance between the three of us.

We danced and had such a good time that we nearly forgot to cut the cake. Suddenly, Poppy came rolling it outside on the stand. "I don't know about the rest of you, but I'm a little hungry."

The crowd cheered, and Nathaniel and I were pushed forward to cut it.

I looked up at Nathaniel as we both cut into the cake. There was a gleam in his eyes, accompanied by debate.

But when we both lifted our pieces, there was no question.

We both shoved it into each other's faces with a wicked grin, a shriek, and a laugh.

The hour was stretching late and as the party wound down, individuals started to come say goodbye and leave. So, Nathaniel and I grabbed our bags and Peter took them out to the car, parked out front, decorated to the max, JUST MARRIED scrawled across the windows.

Our friends and family lined up along the sidewalk. And hand in hand, Nathaniel ran out the doors, through a corridor of sparklers, waving at the well-wishers.

Nathaniel opened my door for me, and I carefully climbed inside, tucking my full dress around me so that it wouldn't get shut in the door. He climbed into the driver's seat and closed his door behind him.

"Off we go, Mrs. Nightingale?" he asked.

The hunger was instantly in my eyes as I met his in the dark. I simply leaned forward, cupping my hand behind his head, and brought his lips to mine. "Drive fast."

After all the bouncing we had done in the last year and a half, I wasn't entirely anxious to travel to some far away place for our honeymoon. Instead, we had opted for a private cabin in the woods, only a forty-minute drive from Nightingale Academy.

There was a trail of candles leading up to the front door when we arrived and parked out front. They flickered and glowed in the dark, romantic and inviting.

Nathaniel climbed out and walked around to my door. He opened it for me, giving me a hand to help me climb out.

Together, we stared at the adorable little cabin.

Two years. That was how long Nathaniel and I had known each other. Nearly two years we'd been in love.

We'd fought. We'd broken up. We'd been unsure of what the future would bring.

But here we were.

Together.

Husband and wife.

Nathaniel took my hand, offering a soft expression. Together, dressed in our wedding clothes, we walked up to the door. And when we reached it, a coy smile formed on Nathaniel's face. He bent and scooped me off my feet.

I squealed in surprise, even though I shouldn't have been. Nathaniel was exceptionally traditional.

He grabbed the doorknob, twisted, and pushed it open.

Holding my gaze, he walked across the threshold. I leaned forward, cupping my hand around the back of his neck, and brought his lips to mine.

That was all it took. I didn't even glance around the space to see where we were or if we were actually alone.

Nathaniel set me down as our lips grew more frantic. My hands came to the lapels of his jacket and I roughly yanked it back and down his arms. He fought with it the rest of the way, flinging it into the corner as his hands joined mine in unbuttoning his shirt.

I huffed air into his mouth, but our lips never separated as a smile crossed both of our faces. My hands slid over Nathaniel's chest as he pulled his shirt off, letting it, too, fall to the floor.

His lips trailed down my throat as he turned me in

place and his fingers went to the laces across my back. He didn't seem intimidated or confused by them. Adeptly, he pulled in all the right places, loosening them with an impressive speed.

Finally, I felt it come loose enough for me to escape. Holding the dress to my chest, I turned in place, my eyes rising to meet Nathaniel's.

The frenzy in his eyes calmed for a moment. I wondered if he was nervous, too. Because I was nervous. This was a first, for both of us.

But it was with each other. It could never be anything but perfect.

So, with confidence, I let the dress pool to the floor.

I watched the hunger reignite and spark in Nathaniel's eyes as they took all of me in. They trailed over the strapless, white bra I wore, and the flimsy panties that hugged my curves.

"Thor's hammer, I love you," Nathaniel whispered as he laced his fingers into my hair and brought my lips back to his. His hands were greedy, and he didn't wait two more seconds before he hoisted me up. My legs wrapped around his waist, and I relished in the skin to skin contact between us.

He walked us across the room. I was faintly aware of a bedroom, but I couldn't focus. Not when Nathaniel's lips trailed down the front of my neck, down my chest.

I heaved in desperate breaths, my head tilting back as his hands overwhelmed me, touching me everywhere. My hands knotted into his hair, trying to keep myself upright.

More, more, more, my body screamed, ready to cross this threshold, with him.

Nathaniel carried me through the bedroom door and toppled me onto the bed.

CHAPTER TWENTY-TWO

EIGHT MONTHS LATER

"Everyone is going to be sharing a bedroom this semester," I said as I looked over the roster. There were nine new names, every one of them a first semester student.

"The reality is that we could fit four students per bedroom, if we really had to," Mary-Beth said as she looked down at the map of the house, with all of its bedrooms. "At least we aren't to that yet."

I shook my head. "It won't be long. You're increasing our class size by twenty percent every semester, and Borden is growing us by at least ten. Come this time next year, we won't be able to accept every student we find."

"Kind of an incredible problem to have, isn't it?" Mary-Beth said with a smile.

I shook my head. "It's...it's almost hard to believe this is our problem. A few years ago, it felt like we were alone. And now we have eleven graduates, a third of whom are becoming teachers now."

It was true. In the beginning, I'd set up the academy to be a three-semester schedule to teach mages the basics of magic. Our first two sets of mages had already graduated, the third would graduate in just eleven weeks. And there were already two classes behind them.

Julie, Alexandra, and Thomas had decided to stay on and help us teach here at the academy. They would take over the first semester classes, with Nathaniel and I continuing the second and third semester student classes.

Mary-Beth continued working as our recruiter. Poppy and Borden still traveled full time, looking for what new mages they could find, scouring libraries wherever they went.

I kept hoping that something might spark between them. But it never had.

They would both find their people. Someday.

"I think you're right," Nathaniel said as he walked into the living room where we were working. "We need to start on the expansion."

I pulled out the big sheet of paper from the bottom of the stack of pages before me. On it was a map of the grounds of Nightingale Academy. There was the house. The garage. The pool that was currently being restored.

But in red ink, there were plans for the new structures we'd been debating for four months now.

One was a dorm building. We could fit a building large enough to have twenty-four bedrooms and twelve bathrooms. On the main floor, there was a mess kitchen and housing for a cook and housekeeper. If we moved the students out there, that would keep room in the main house for the teachers. And as Nathaniel and I got older and grew into a family with children someday, it would give us a little bit of separation between our family and the students.

The other building was a large gym. The main house was already showing signs of wear, having us use it for practice over and over every day. Someday someone was going to make a mistake doing a fire-starting spell and blow the place up. In the gym, we would have plenty of space and there would be nothing to hurt.

"Call Brent," I said with a nod. I felt good about the decision. And really, it was such a blessing to have to make this decision. To outgrow this mansion of a house and need an expansion. "Have him file the permits. Let's get him working on it as soon as he is available."

Nathaniel smiled, laying a hand on my knee for a moment, before he got up to go and search for the number of the contractor who had restored this house for us.

"Look at you, Mama Nightingale," Mary-Beth teased gently. "Expanding the nest."

I smiled at her teasing. I truly loved it. Teaching magic. Meeting new students. Forming this community with those who passed through our doors.

Just then, the front one opened and in walked my mother, and our latest guest, Agnes McGregor.

"I don't know how you have the patience for it," Agnes said in her strong Scottish accent. "All those years of teaching freshmen. I would go mad within the first thirty minutes."

"Patience is a practiced virtue," Mom said as the two women wandered in and headed for the kitchen.

Two months ago, we received a letter from Agnes, asking if she could come to the academy and see what we were doing here. We had immediately responded that yes, she could, and bought her a flight. Agnes was a direct cousin of mine, being a McGregor. Even though she herself was locked, she knew as much as possible about her ancestry and what they could do. When we'd run into her in Scotland, she'd been so helpful to us. We owed her a great debt of gratitude.

So, she had been here for the past two weeks, fascinated with everything we could do. We'd shown her real magic. She'd had endless questions and watched for hours as we lived our normal lives, with the assistance of magic. We'd even gotten to be tourists with her, taking her to all the local vacationer places. She'd been entirely overwhelmed with the massiveness that was Boston.

"Oh, Margot," Mom said as she pulled back from the fridge. "There's a great big man standing outside your house. Big beard. Kind of intimidating looking. He looks a little lost, but he keeps looking at the house like he's expecting something."

My brow furrowed and I looked at Mary-Beth with confusion. "One of the new students? They are supposed to arrive in the next hour."

Mary-Beth shrugged. "That doesn't sound like anyone I sent letters to. Maybe he's just homeless?" she suggested.

"I don't think so," Agnes said. "Too clean kept. Just looks kind of lost."

Borden passed through just then, and curious, he crossed to the front door and opened it.

"Well, I wouldn't have believed it if I weren't seeing him," Borden said, his tone full of wonder. I got up and crossed to his side, looking out.

"Otto?" I said, hardly believing my eyes.

The giant German man stood at the gates, staring at the house, looking utterly lost.

Borden and I both walked out and made our way down the driveway to meet him.

"I didn't know why I felt compelled to come," he said. "I just knew that I had to come to the states, to this town, and look for a house on the water."

I opened the gate and it swung wide, revealing the poor German man.

Borden and I had spent an entire summer in Europe, traveling all around, searching for magical books. While in Germany, we were told about a placed called Hexenhaus, which was owned by a man who claimed to know lots of crazy things about magic.

There we had found Otto Huber.

He knew our history. He knew about the witch hunts. He knew about magic.

He thought he was the descendant of a necromancer. But when we tested him, we were shocked to find that he had no mage blood.

He had dozens of real magic books though, as well as maps and crystals we still didn't understand the use of.

It was the guiltiest I'd ever felt. But Borden and I had taken his real magic things and left him money in exchange. We'd messed with his mind so that he wouldn't be bothered when he realized some of his things were missing.

But I had also told him to seek us out someday. That we would be happy to talk to him.

"I think I remember the both of you," he said as his eyes flicked between us. "You came to see me in Germany."

"That's right," I said, nodding as I smiled. I was so happy he was here. "Otto, would you please come inside?"

Just then, a woman walked up the sidewalk, looking at the house in an unsure way. There was another man just behind her.

"Is this...is this the Nightingale Academy?" the young woman asked.

"It is," I said, lifting my chin and smiling at them. A car pulled up and two young adults climbed out, obviously siblings. "Why don't you all come inside with me?"

"How is that for timing?" Borden asked as we turned, and everyone began following us. "How much do you plan on telling the human?"

I sometimes worried about Borden. Because he separated himself from those who couldn't do magic. As if they were another species. His world was growing smaller and tighter, despite his travels.

"He already knows pretty much all of it," I said. "He's just never seen proof that he isn't crazy."

"You don't think it's too much of a risk?" Borden asked as we walked up the porch steps.

"I've been in his mind, don't forget that," I said as we walked into the living room. Seeing the crowd, Nathaniel came to join us, Khan standing obediently at his side. "He's a good man. I do trust him."

Borden gave an acknowledging noise, though it didn't sound exactly like he agreed. But he wouldn't fight me.

They didn't need to be told to come down. They knew the time, and the way this worked. Julie, Alexandra, and Thomas came down the stairs, watching the group grow as more of them arrived.

I reached out and took Nathaniel's hand as we watched them gather.

"This will be our biggest semester yet," Nathaniel noted. "I got in touch with Brent. He said he can get started on the expansion in two weeks. Thinks he'll have it completed in ten months."

"Good," I nodded. "We're going to need it."

They all came. It wasn't always the case. Occasionally, Mary-Beth sent out the invitation and they went completely ignored. They thought it was a joke or that we were crazy. Which was fine.

But others wanted to believe.

They wanted magic to be real.

So, they took a leap of faith. They went to the address at the time appointed. They came to see what would happen.

And they ended up staying. They committed and they learned.

They became family.

All nine of them stood there in my living room, looking nervous and confused, but curious.

"Thank you for coming," Nathaniel said as Mary-Beth closed the front door. "We know you all aren't entirely sure why you're here. But I can tell you that it is because of your ancestry. Your blood. You're here to learn what was once lost in the past."

I squeezed Nathaniel's hand, utterly elated, the same as I was every first day of a new semester.

"Welcome to the Nightingale Academy," I said, lifting my voice so they all could hear. "We're so glad you're here."

THE END

ABOUT THE AUTHOR

Keary Taylor is the USA TODAY bestselling author of over thirty titles, encompassing paranormal, sci-fi, and contemporary romance. She grew up along the foothills of the Rocky Mountains where, from a young age, she started creating imaginary worlds and daring characters who always fell in love. She now lives on a tiny island in the Pacific Northwest with her husband and their two children. She continues to have an overactive imagination that frequently keeps her up at night.

To learn more about Keary, please visit her website: www.kearytaylor.com.

- facebook.com/kearytaylor
- twitter.com/kearytaylor
- instagram.com/authorkearytaylor

Printed in Great Britain
by Amazon